A Jonathan Chamb...

BLOOD SAND AND CREAM TEAS

Best wishes

David Munday

DAVID MUNDAY

Copyright © 2024 by David Munday

ISBN: 9798339723851

All rights reserved.

No portion of this book may be reproduced in any form without written permission from the publisher or author, except as permitted by U.K. copyright law.

Contents

Acknowledgments		V
1.	Chapter One	1
2.	Chapter Two	8
3.	Chapter Three	23
4.	Chapter Four	30
5.	Chapter Five	40
6.	Chapter Six	46
7.	Chapter Seven	56
8.	Chapter Eight	66
9.	Chapter Nine	77
10.	Chapter Ten	85

11.	Chapter Eleven	99
12.	Chapter Twelve	106
13.	Chapter Thirteen	112
14.	Chapter Fourteen	117
15.	Chapter Fifteen	127
16.	Chapter Sixteen	137
17.	Chapter Seventeen	145
18.	Chapter Eighteen	155
19.	Chapter Nineteen	163
20.	Chapter Twenty	172
21.	Chapter Twenty-One	184
22.	Chapter Twenty-Two	193
23.	Chapter Twenty-Three	197
24.	Chapter Twenty-Four	211
Epilogue		216
About The Author		222

Acknowledgments

I would like to thank my wonderful wife, Aude, and many friends and family who have taken the trouble to suggest improvements. I'd also like to thank Alex for his help and support in making this book possible.

Chapter One

The King holds in demesne Skandelburgh. Then at 5 hides, now for 4 hides. Land for use by 6 ploughs. In demesne 1 plough and 6 villans and 1 bordar with 3 ploughs. There are 2 slaves and 1 site in Bectoun and 1 fishery worth 7s and 6d and 20 acres of meadow. Woodland for 80 pigs. At the time of King Edward it was worth 90s, and afterwards and now it is worth 50s.
(Extract from Domesday Book, 1086)

Soaked in sweat, Jonathan lay gasping as nightmare images flashed through his mind. His throat was dry, as bile rose in his gullet. It had been the same ever since he was ten, when his uncle and aunt had taken him in as a frightened child. Despite them treating him as their own, pouring love and affection over him, every time he thought he was over it, the dream would return with a vengeance.

There had been so many emotions to contend with: anger and bitterness, a desire for revenge, despair and even thoughts of suicide, and his adoptive parents had guided him through it all. He felt a rush of affection for them and resolved to visit them again soon. He got out of bed and stumbled to the basin where he gulped down a glass of water.

Compelled to go downstairs to the living room, he stared at the framed photo of his parents. There they were standing either side of a camel. In the background was the desert under a deep blue sky. His parents were laughing, not a care in the world. Those were happy days: games of cricket in the back yard, trips out into the desert in a 4x4, and picnics beneath those sandstone hills, eroded into grotesque shapes by a thousand years of weathering.

He opened a drawer in the bureau and picked up a letter his parents had written to him when he was nine. Perhaps sensing the danger they were in, the letter had come with strict instructions that it only be opened after their deaths.

Dear Jonathan

We hope you will never have to read this but if you do, we want you to know how much we love you and would encourage you to be brave and not let our deaths stop you from living life to the full.

Work hard at school, get a university education and find a career that suits you; whether your wish is to follow your dad and have an army career or follow a less active profession and take a university degree. We know how much you love history. Not many little boys we know would happily spend hours in a museum without complaining! We know you will do well whatever path you choose.

But more importantly, try to live by the principles that we have both tried to follow: value every human being, help anyone who needs it, and be faithful to your friends. Appreciate beauty: whether in a sunset or a landscape, in a painting or, perhaps, even in your friends.

You are a cheerful happy boy with such a passion for cricket. Keep that up and one day you will play at Lords!

Finally find belief: a faith that is loving, compassionate and drives you to do great things- and may God go with you.

Your loving parents,

Edward and Maria

Tears welled up in his eyes as he read. He remembered his dad: tall and proud, a man who stuck firmly to his principles. He recalled how he had been told off for throwing a stone at a pigeon in the back yard – "*treat every living creature as you would want to be treated yourself*", his father had said and this principle became embedded in his consciousness. His mother, warm and loving, could always find just the right words of comfort for his youthful distress; she encouraged him to do everything to the best of his ability, praised his successes, and somehow managed to help him through failure so he could learn from it, and never be discouraged.

Had he followed his parents' advice? Once he had gained access to his trust fund when he had turned 18, had got a reasonable education, had read history at Oxford and travelled the world, he decided to settle in Skandlebury. Two years later and now in his mid-twenties the pace of life had slowed. He was bored.

He had taken up cricket as his parents had advised, but did he believe in anything? How could a loving God allow such a dreadful tragedy? Whenever he thought of God a blank numbness seemed to descend upon him. Yet, if there was no God, why was there such beauty in the world? This strange divide in the world between the extraordinary beauty and symmetry of creation and the despair and misery that afflicted mankind, baffled him. His philosophy professor at Oxford had not helped either. To him, God was a convenient construct of primitive minds and religion would die out as the world became more educated. His friend, Mike Jones, had tried to convince him along similar lines. Their efforts had left him totally uncertain, and the vicar of St. Michael's, although relating to him confidently the message of the Bible and redemption through Christ's sacrificial death, always became rather vague when trying to explain why God allowed such dreadful evil in the present day.

As to the qualities his parents had urged him to adopt - well... that was for someone else to judge. He certainly seemed to have inherited his parents' sense of beauty and love of the countryside. Overall, however, he felt miserable and worthless at not living up to what his parents had expected of him. How could he possibly? What was he doing with his life now? The answer came to him, bleak and final: nothing.

After shutting the letter back in the drawer, he returned to his bedroom, hesitating just for a moment before changing into his running kit. He opened the front door and was soon speeding down School Lane towards the village of Skandlebury. Outside, though still dark, the birds had begun to sing and the sky had lightened. There was not a soul to be seen. Expending his energies on vigorous exercise always seemed to help him recover from his bouts of depression. Maybe it was the adrenalin boost it gave him along with the sense of physical wellbeing.

The village of Skandlebury, his home now for two years, slumbered in the grey light of dawn. Despite its somewhat unfortunate name there appeared to be no dark side to Skandlebury. Unless you include petty disagreements, which are common in all small communities most people got on extremely well, and if they didn't, they didn't make a fuss about it. People kept a friendly eye on elderly neighbours and a transport system was available for the less mobile, so they could keep hospital appointments or visit sick relatives. There was a slew of social events such as bingo in the village hall, a walking club and a reading group. Indeed Skandlebury, was a happy place, at ease with itself as it nestled beneath the tower of the half ruined Norman castle.

Not a sound could be heard as he quickened his pace around the village green and past the pub which he would later visit for a pint and a ploughman's, and then along the road towards Beckton, the county town of Beckshire. Normally, when it was lighter he would run through the woods which loomed up to his left, but so as not to risk a sprained ankle, he continued along the deserted road, past the Council estate, and out into open country. Although still a little shaken, he felt strong, full of the vitality of youth.

He would often have his best thoughts when running, and he had soon firmly resolved, as he had done on so many occasions, not to let the terrorist thugs who killed his parents win. That meant to do his parents proud by making the most of his life. By the time he was running home he felt much more positive.

A vigorous shower and a breakfast of toast and coffee followed. He felt he was just killing time until the pub opened and should be doing something constructive. He picked up his newspaper and sat down on his bright red sofa. He liked to keep his brain sharp with the cryptic crossword. His ginger tom cat, Sir Lancelot, ever on the lookout for a vacant lap, seized the opportunity that Jonathan's presence afforded and settled down purring. Jonathan stroked him affectionately. (He had a huge affection for the cat whom his uncle had given him as a kitten, not long after the death of his parents, and this rather lazy and elderly feline had been a tremendous source of comfort to him in those early days.)

As he opened the paper, he noticed a headline and stiffened: *Bomb Factory found in London,* but it was the subheading that made him sit up: *OAK terrorists suspected; two arrested.* So Octol Al Kfara were active in London. He stifled a feeling of panic. They could not be after him surely – that was ridiculous. They were, after all, into activities which, in their twisted minds, were of far more importance than chasing after a survivor of an old assassination attempt. He was aware this terrorist group were meticulous in taking vengeance on their enemies, and though he had been just ten when his parents died, they would view him as such, as he had relayed important information to the authorities. *But surely*, he thought, *they had bigger plans than just to chase after him.*

For what felt like hours he tried in vain to concentrate. Sir Lancelot slept on unaware of his master's tension. Eventually Jonathan gently pushed him off his lap. "Sorry old chap, gotta go."

Chapter Two

Jonathan Chambers took a sip of beer and placed it, somewhat absent-mindedly, back on the beermat. Sitting at the polished oak bar of the Puss-in-Boots pub – the only one in Skandlebury – he allowed the liquid to swirl around his mouth before swallowing it. On the adjacent stool sat a small round man with bright, brown birdlike eyes, which were a sharp contrast to his light blue oil-stained overalls.

"You know, Bert," Jonathan said, "I could really do with some excitement. Life's becoming too predictable. Every day I get up, have breakfast, read the paper, tidy up a bit, and then come here for a pint and a ploughman's. Okay, I might go for a jog and keep fit, but I can't help wondering, if this is all there is to life." He took another sip of his beer. "It's probably just an attack of the pre-cricket season blues."

Bert Wright sighed. This wasn't the first time Jonathan had said something like this and Bert was getting tired of listening. "Look Jon, just cut it out will you? Life is what you make of it. You have everything going for you, you don't even have to work to make ends meet. Unlike you, I don't have any inherited wealth to fall back on. It's mending cars every day – hard physical work. I'd swap your place for mine any day. Only difference is I wouldn't complain, and I'd make sure I went out into the world and enjoyed myself. Why don't you? Just go for it. You're only young once."

"That's just it," sighed Jonathan, taking a much larger gulp of beer, " I'm happy with village life. I don't want to travel the world again. The problem is right now, the only thing worth looking forward to is next week's start to the cricket season."

"Well, I suppose that's one thing you're good at," said Bert. "Your left arm spin is legendary and people still talk about the way you played Pobbleton's fast bowler last season."

Jonathan perked up a bit and pushed a stray lock of fair hair off his forehead. "Legendary." He liked that. "Yes, I am rather good, aren't I?" he laughed.

Bert smiled. He wasn't going to put up with Jonathan's whining any more.

Jonathan ordered them both another pint and Bert gulped his down quickly. Wiping his mouth with the back of his hand, he made for the door. "I'm one of the world's workers," he said. Jonathan showed little sign of having heard though, his attention elsewhere.

Jonathan, meanwhile, had heard Bert's comment but had chosen to ignore it. His mind wandered to the sumptuousness of the pub's interior. Its dark furniture had been there since Victorian times and the oak bar and smoke blackened beams from the time when King Henry was dissolving monasteries. Above the hearth, where a log fire burned, staving off the spring chill, were markings, hexafoils, and crosses carved in the dark oak, hundreds of years old, made by superstitious farm workers to ward off witches. The pub was all about stability in an ever-changing world, and to Jonathan this was important. It had been his second home for several years now, and life without this bastion of British culture was unthinkable. In short, the pub was balm to his troubled soul and, for just a few precious hours, helped him forget.

Many of the faces in the pub were familiar. There was Mike Jones a fellow cricketer, he was an atheist and proud father of hyperactive twin boys; Bessie who worked in the tea shop, and Claire, who sometimes helped there too. Currently they were sipping white wine at a table by the window in the company of Claire's father, the vicar. He was an earnest man who enjoyed a pint or two – it helped him interact with his parishioners... or so the rumours went. He'd not long replaced the aged incumbent who'd passed away last Christmas whilst conducting the Christingle service. The tale of the former's passing was, in itself, very entertaining. The parish church of St Michael and All Angels had been lit by candles that night as part of the service and, due to the general gloom, it had been quite a few moments after the conclusion of a particularly lengthy carol that the vicar's body had been spotted slumped in the pulpit.

The pub was usually busier in the evenings, but for Thursday lunchtime the numbers today were surprisingly good. This would please host Gary Landsman who ran the pub with his wife, Coral, and son Billy. Coral was the chef with a talent for turning a humble traditional English meal into a work of art. Many people would forsake their local hostelries in the surrounding villages to savour her melt-in-the-mouth steak and kidney pie or her dish of Beckshire sausages with onion gravy.

It was as he sat observing the lives of his fellow villagers, meditating over his pint that Jonathan first noticed the stranger in the bar. He came into Jonathan's line of vision as the former rose from his seat and walked towards him. He was a tall man with a thin, tanned face, slightly hooked nose, and high cheekbones. His hair was receding, and Jonathan thought he looked to be around forty years old. The stranger wore a loose-fitting tweed jacket and woollen tie, much like a sheep farmer on his way to market. There was something vaguely familiar about him. He had a drink in one hand and a beige folder under his arm.

"Hi," the man said, "I'm David Sims. Detective Inspector Sims." He produced his official ID. "I couldn't help overhearing your conversation and I might have a proposition for you but I need to make sure I've got my facts straight. You're a keen cricketer, right?"

"Yes," Jonathan replied, "I play for Skandlebury."

"Good," said the detective, "and you have time on your hands? If so, I have something you could help me with. Police business but strictly off the books."

"You might say life's a bit slow at the moment."

The detective was silent for a moment as if thinking. "So you'd be open to completing a little task for us?" he asked.

"I might be," Jon replied. He was still wondering where he had come across this man before.

"And where were you educated?"

"Eton and Oxford," Jonathan said, "I'm the proud owner of an MA in history."

The detective made no comment on Jonathan's prestigious education.

"Do you like puzzles?" he asked.

"What sort of puzzles?" Jonathan was taken aback at this rather random line of questioning.

"Sudoku, crosswords, whodunits, that sort of thing. In short, do you like to solve mysteries?"

"Well yes, I suppose so," said Jonathan slowly, "I do crosswords, particularly cryptic ones and the newspaper puzzle page occasionally. Oh, and I read detective stories if that's what you mean. Although you'd be more likely to find me in front of the TV watching a Miss Marple box set."

D I Sims nodded. "Good, good. You obviously have an enquiring mind. Another pint?"

Jonathan accepted, wondering if Sims was ever going to get to the point. He didn't have to wait long.

Sims took a long sip of his drink and directed his gaze to Jonathan.

"At Beckton Nick," Sims began, "we have a serious problem. We're horrendously under resourced and with our targets as they are…" he paused, "…well, we have every motivation not to delve too deeply into cases that on the surface appear straight forward. Did you hear about the recent death of Captain Frobisher?"

"How could I not? He fell from the hayloft in his barn and smashed his head open on the corner of an old plough. It was in all the local papers and gossip fodder for a while round here. Terrible tragedy. Such a good cricketer too. Why? What does that have to do with me?"

The detective shrugged. "It has nothing at all to do with you, unless you killed him". Sims laughed, "which wouldn't be the most bizarre theory we've heard. You may recall, however, that a verdict of accidental death was recorded. However, I don't think it was accidental at all."

Intrigued, Jonathan took a sip of his pint as he recalled some of the more far-fetched theories bandied about soon after the Captain's death. One of his personal favourites was that Captain Frobisher had killed himself following a poor run of cricket form. Other theories surrounded Mrs Frobisher having killed him for his money or because she suspected him of having an affair. What was odd, now he came to think of it, was that everyone had believed there to be an element of foul play, including, it would appear, the police. Theories involving aliens and that he was a spy were quickly discounted of course, but it was puzzling that no one except the Frobishers themselves, and possibly a farm worker, were on the premises at the time of his death. This limited the pool of potential killers and pointed more towards accident or suicide.

"What makes you think there's more to it?" asked Jonathan.

"Two reasons," the detective replied. "Firstly, a white car was seen driving off at speed near the scene of the tragedy by a passing cyclist and all efforts to trace this car have failed."

"And the second reason?"

"The captain writes a blog. In it, he said words to the effect that 'cricket was no longer a gentleman's game and he thought there were people in cricket fanatical enough to kill to get their own way.'" The detective paused a moment, eyes darting around the pub's interior, making sure, Jonathan surmised, that they could not be overheard.

"I understand from a member of the club," Sims continued, "that the Captain was about to be told they were taking him out of the first team to make way for a retired County player, someone who could guarantee Bellhinton Cricket Club would win the village trophy this season. With Frobisher dead there'd be no chance of him getting in the way, thus his passing was a convenient solution. However the comment may just have been an exaggeration."

Bellhinton was a smaller village about two miles to the south. Bellhinton and Skandlebury often joined together for events, including the annual Easter fete. There was a fierce but largely friendly rivalry between them, particularly over who should get the cricket trophy and to have a player of county standard was a tremendous boost to Bellhinton's chances of winning the honour for the first time in several years.

"So, you think his death was in some way connected to his position in the cricket team. It's a bit far fetched, isn't it?" Jonathan said, "I mean who kills over a game of cricket?"

The detective smiled. "As I said Mr Frobisher's comment was probably not a serious one. According to his associates, Edwin Frobisher was a harmless fellow. In retirement he'd been devoted to his hobby farm and was a stalwart of the cricket team; however, we have reports that his form as an opening batsman was in question. When ex-professional cricketer Alan Hardy arrived in the village, the Bellhinton team couldn't believe their luck. They were keen to get rid of Frobisher and start Hardy at the beginning of the season. Frobisher's death could be considered an unfortunate coincidence, but I don't believe in coincidences and certainly not fortuitous ones."

Jonathan nodded, his curiosity piqued. "Why are you sharing this with me?"

"Well," Sims said, "you're deep into the local cricketing world so you could carry out covert investigations better than anyone on the police force. You seem a likeable easy going fellow, the sort people take into their confidence, and I'm led to believe you don't need money, which definitely works for us. There would be no payment for your help as it would be strictly 'off the record.' The case was officially closed- too quickly in my view - but as I say several of us in the force have our doubts, so would like to give the investigation one last shot. We think that someone on the inside might find out more than us. We don't need you to be an amateur detective, just keep us informed of any whispers. You know, ask a few questions over a pint, that sort of thing. Maybe you could get to know the Bellhinton Cricket Club members, or perhaps even join them. There can't be too many demon left arm spinners who can hold a bat, knocking around."

Jonathan preened at the detective's compliment and then frowned. "I can't be disloyal to my own team, and we start next week. I also know many of the Bellhinton cricketers. One or two live in Skandlebury but play for Bellhinton because they couldn't get a place in our team. I can't see that talking to them is going to help. If there's a link, they're not going to tell me."

The detective smiled, unperturbed by Jonathan's argument. "They wouldn't all be party to a conspiracy, if indeed there was one, and there are bound to be dissenters. If you can find the slightest hint of a plot, all you need to do is tell me. But, just to be clear, that is the only basis on which you're to be involved. If Frobisher's death was indeed murder, you could get yourself in real danger. When do you play Bellhinton next?"

"This weekend, actually," Jonathan replied, "Saturday fixture. A friendly. Sunday league cricket starts the following week. Pobbleton are our first league fixture, then Crainscombe."

"Oh yes – Pobbleton are the team with the fast bowler."

Jonathan grinned. "Craig Westall. I knocked him all over the shop. Turned 5 for 35 into 250 for 8 in 50 overs. I contributed 107 before being caught behind, and Tony Topliss 64."

D I Sims looked impressed. "Yes, I like cricket myself, played for Cambridge Uni but not their main team."

"Really?" Back on his favourite subject Jonathan was infinitely more comfortable, though his mind continued to whirr. In the background thoughts, theories, and possibilities crowded his brain. "You should try out for Bellhinton or Skandlebury," he suggested, knowing that both sides were always in need of good players. Plus, it would keep the detective close.

"I may well do that," Sims replied. "Maybe your team. I hear the captain is retiring...Do you meet at the bar after games? I need you to ask a few questions, that's all."

Jonathan nodded, "We do." The social side of the game was something he particularly enjoyed. "We're a pretty friendly lot," he continued. "Drinking at the bar is nearly as important as the match itself and after the annual friendly we have a bit of a party. It's a tradition."

"See if you can find anything out, then," Sims suggested, "people talk more freely with a beer in their hand. Find out what they were doing over the weekend of Frobisher's death. There was a spring fair and children's Easter egg hunt at Bellhinton on the same weekend so use that as your way in. Ask them if they were there. If not, why not? I'm convinced several people didn't tell me all they knew."

Sims placed his empty beer glass on the bar before passing Jonathan the tan, manila folder he'd been carrying ever since he entered the pub.

"In the meantime," he said, "I want you to read this. It summarises the case and there are witness statements you might find helpful. Let me know what you think. Oh, and here's my card, call me any time."

The detective turned to leave but before he did, he glanced back at Jonathan. Their eyes met and once again he had the overwhelming conviction they'd met before. But where?

He watched the detective's departing form as he ruminated on their conversation. *Was it usual for a detective to ask an unqualified member of the public to work undercover? Was Sims who he said he was?* Something about him didn't add up. Jonathan knew all the detectives at Beckton Station on account of attending a police function with DI Roberts's daughter last year. He was certain that Sims had not been among the people he'd met. With a shake of his head, he drained his glass, resolving that the first investigation he would undertake would be a little digging into the mysterious DI Sims. There was definitely something familiar about the other man's face. Something from Jonathan's past. His mind ran through school friends, teachers, and people he'd met through his aunt and uncle, but he could not place Sims.

Bidding farewell to Gary Landsman, who was standing behind the bar, he headed for the door, blinking as bright sunlight flooded his eyes. It took a moment for his vision to adjust but, when it had, Jonathan was comforted to see that Skandlebury remained in fine, if somewhat clichéd form. There was a row of giant cherry trees adjacent to the Puss in Boots, like candy-floss soldiers standing to attention. Bluebells peeped timidly out of the ditch that ran along the hedgerow, yet to be in full bloom. Cottages with thatched roofs, green with moss, clustered around the parish church, its spire soaring high into the eggshell blue sky. Just visible on a mound beyond the green, was the stump of a Norman keep glimpsed above the cottage roofs like a broken tooth. From far away came the sound of the village primary school children at lunchtime play. A tractor was mowing the expansive green which was artfully framed by a ditch and horse chestnut trees. The heady mix of diesel with damp, newly mown grass was intoxicating.

Jonathan loved the countryside. Ever since he'd settled back in England he'd felt a connection to the rural scene. It had played a key part in the healing process following the loss of his parents. Long walks with his aunt and uncle had been soothing, although these became more solitary affairs as he got older. Alone he could allow the peace and quiet to steal into his soul, a balm on raw and open wounds. Crowds bothered him, and the bustle of city life was to be endured rather than enjoyed. He loved Skandlebury now and couldn't imagine living anywhere else; however, he had recently become restless. Perhaps his mental scars were finally healing, and he needed a more solid purpose in life. Maybe, Jonathan reflected, investigating this case was just what he was looking for. That and the new cricket season, of course.

Crossing the village green, he passed the reed fringed duck pond, and his eyes were immediately drawn to the dearly familiar outline of the cricket pavilion on the right. This was a newish building built of red brick with a slate roof which stood proudly over the cricket pitch, this having been carved out of adjacent woodland some one hundred years ago. The land belonged to the Duke of Crainscombe who had helped raise the funds for the new pavilion. This building, which replaced a rather dilapidated wooden construction, now housed a bar, kitchen, and changing facilities, and had become the de facto village hall.

As he cut across the green moving away from the cricket ground, the sound of children playing grew louder. Skandlebury Primary School stood on the other side of the road skirting the green, where it joined the appropriately named School Lane. Jonathan crossed the road and entered the lane. Four hundred yards on the right was his cottage, a substantial house dating back to late Tudor times. It was set in grounds of an acre or so, its lawns and flowerbeds immaculately tended by John Bristow, a local gardener. From the front, the house was a vision of Flemish patterned brickwork, wooden joists darkened with age and leaded windows.

He let himself in and collapsed on his squashy red sofa. Low oak beams and whitewashed walls gave the lounge an appropriate olde world feel but in a moment of madness, as he later reflected, Jonathan had hired an interior designer who had added bright, primary colours. The red sofa was cheerfully adorned with yellow cushions and noisy modern art hung on the walls. These flashes of colour, along with the French windows he'd also installed, all gave much needed illumination to an otherwise dark interior. Sir Lancelot, who also contributed in his own small way to the brightness of the lounge, was draped over an armchair. He awoke on Jonathan's arrival and crossed the room to jump on his lap.

With a deep sigh and hardly noticing his cat, Jonathan sank deeper into the sofa his mind whirring. Did he want to get involved in what Sims had suggested? Was it really possible that Captain Frobisher had been murdered? Did he even want to find out?

******

Elsewhere, Jonathan's friend Bert was on his mobile phone.

"Hi. It's Bert. You spoke to Jon?"

On the other end of the line D I Sims chuckled. "Oh yes, and he bought the whole thing. He's a very nice chap but a bit gullible. Personally, I thought the cricketing motive was weak but I'm confident he'll take on the case. I don't think he'll content himself with just talk at the cricket club. He'll take it on as a project."

"Well, let's hope it will occupy that dreamy brain of his for a while," Bert said, laughing, "and then I can have my lunchtime pint in peace."

Chapter Three

A week earlier, Jonathan had gone to visit his Uncle Bill and Aunt Sarah.

He frequently visited them because they alone knew what he had been through. He'd felt particularly in the mood for a visit due to the anniversary of his parents' deaths. He'd known the visit would follow a predictable pattern: long walks with his uncle, his aunt showing him family photos, and being spoilt with delicious meals.

They lived in Upper Tiddenham not far from where he'd grown up, in a cosy cottage on the edge of the village. It was more a small hamlet really, comprised of a row of old, whitewashed cottages, and a scattering of residences that had been built more recently. It did boast a church though, part of the benefice of Tiddenham, and services were held there once a month. The cottage in which his aunt and uncle lived was opposite the church. Jonathan's bedroom was at the rear, however, which meant he was afforded a splendid view of rolling countryside and distant hills which formed part of the Beckshire downs.

His uncle, William, much like Edward, Jon's father, had worked for the government. In fact, it had been Edward who had urged William to apply for the post in the intelligence services that he subsequently held for most of his working life. William had only been retired for a few years, but this didn't stop him from being frequently called upon by the government for advice. It is said you never really retire from being a spy. Both William and Edward had been similarly employed meaning Jonathan's uncle could empathise with what Jonathan had gone through . When Jonathan had been so cruelly orphaned, at the tender age of ten, it had seemed only natural that his aunt and uncle would take him in and raise him, alongside their own two daughters.

Because the weather had been mostly cold, windy and wet, he'd spent a lot of time curled up on the sofa reading detective novels or watching box sets. A roaring fire had kept him company and saw off the chill.

Jonathan and his uncle had only managed one walk, when the rain had eased a little, and it had been one of Jonathan's favourites, to the top of Upway Hill, where stood the remains of a Stone Age fort. There had been a short and vicious skirmish during the English Civil Wars here and the victorious Royalist cavalry had chased fleeing Roundhead horsemen down the impossibly steep slope causing their end in a lifeless bloody heap at the bottom. The views from the top were panoramic and, on a fine day, one could make out the church spire of Skandlebury.

It had been on the Wednesday, the last full day of Jonathan's visit that his uncle had received a rather disturbing telephone call. Jonathan had just eaten one of his aunt's excellent full English breakfasts and was ensconced on the sofa reading. Outside the rain had been drilling down and a vicious easterly gale had been howling through the cottage's ancient eaves. When the telephone rang in the adjacent hall Uncle William answered it. Jonathan couldn't help but overhear the one-sided conversation.

"Yes, Bob?"

"No, I don't think so."

"He's here with us now. No need to worry".

"Yes, will keep a look out. You say you have everything under control..." His uncle's voice had lowered, but Jonathan was blessed with exceptional hearing. "I hope so for Jon's sake. If anything goes wrong you'll have hell to pay."

Jonathan's mind had raced. How was he involved in something that appeared to put him in danger?

Uncle Bill had then returned to the sitting room, sat in his armchair, and picked up his newspaper and resumed reading as if the call had never taken place.

"Er, Uncle," Jonathan had ventured, "I'm sure you mentioned me during that phone call. I wasn't eavesdropping but you know you prick up your ears when you hear your name mentioned. Am I in some sort of danger?"

His uncle had sighed. "You always did have exceptional hearing, Jon. It's nothing to worry about, but we've had intelligence that members of the terrorist group OAK are in the UK. We're a bit worried they might target you because of their involvement in your parents' murder. Plus, the information you gave us did help us go after them.."

Jon groaned, recalling the newspaper article on their bomb making attempts. "Octol Al Kfara. What are they up to now?"

Bill hesitated before replying. "Nothing we know about yet, but we have our suspicions. The reason for the government's concern was that your cleaning lady phoned the police saying you'd disappeared leaving the front door unlocked."

"Whoops," said Jonathan, "I can be a bit careless with security. It's so quiet where I live. I knew that Mrs. Drewett would be visiting soon after Mike Jones had given me a lift to the station, so I didn't bother. Also I forgot to tell her I was going away. But why should she worry? She knows I can be a scatterbrain."

"The point is," said his uncle, "Your car was still in the drive. The police had asked her to report anything suspicious, and with the front door unlocked, and your car in the drive... well – you see my point."

"Yes, I suppose it did look a bit odd. Why wasn't I told about this before? I would have been more careful."

"I think they didn't want you to get too alarmed. At this stage all we know is that some OAK members may have slipped into this country to join up with other suspected affiliates in London. A bomb making factory was discovered and a couple arrested. They are not talking of course. Personally, I think the security services have overreacted a bit and there's nothing for you to be worried about but, all the same, keep a look out and let me know if you see anything suspicious."

Jonathan had a feeling that he had been holding something back but decided not to pursue the matter.

The rain began to ease, and Jonathan leapt up. "I'm going for a walk. Sod the weather, I'm in danger of getting cabin fever."

"I'll come with you," said Bill, "I could do with stretching my legs, too."

"Well, not if you're busy."

"I'm coming with you, Jon."

"Oh. OK."

"I think we could take that footpath past the church and walk to Lower Tiddenham and maybe grab a bite to eat in the excellent Golden Pear tearooms."

Jonathan nodded and a few moments later the two of them

left the comfort of the cottage and followed the well-trodden path to the side of the church.

On this short walk, Jonathan's uncle barely said a word. It was clear he was preoccupied.

As they approached Lower Tiddenham, his Uncle finally spoke: "You will be careful won't you Jon. Watch out for strangers."

"Aren't you being a bit dramatic?" Jonathan replied, "I mean you said it yourself, we don't know they're after me. I promise I won't be lured into a car by someone offering me sweets," he added, his sarcasm getting the better of him.

"I'm just worried, that's all," his uncle said, "I've been a spy all my life and I still take precautions wherever I go. Just be careful and report anything odd to the police."

Jonathan lay in bed that night, uneasy, worried that somehow his past was returning, not only to haunt his dreams but his waking moments, too. He had wondered what his uncle knew and had been keeping from him. His dreams that night had been of desert sand and blood.

******

In the next room Uncle William had had a restless night too, torn between telling Jonathan more of what he knew, or keep his secrets. In this struggle of loyalties, the secret service eventually won fairly easily.

"Your poor boy," William had murmured to himself as he

rolled over for the umpteenth time, "if only you knew..."

Chapter Four

Jonathan awoke to bright sunlight streaming through a gap in the curtain and the urgent trilling of the doorbell. For a moment he wondered what the noise was, his brain still fogged with sleep. Then the sound registered, and he leapt out of bed, put on his dressing gown and rushed downstairs. He opened the door to a girl who looked to be in her late teens or early twenties.

"Hi," she said looking up at him. She was considerably shorter than he was with a pretty oval face, blue eyes and straw coloured hair, tied back into a ponytail. She wore jodhpurs and a tee-shirt that didn't quite cover her midriff.

"Can I help you?" Jonathan said. Aware of his uncle's advice about trusting strangers he quickly decided, based on nothing but the look of youthful innocence in those large blue eyes, that there was nothing sinister about this young woman.

"My name's Eleanor," she said and, with the directness of youth, plunged straight into her reason for calling. "I want to ask you something. It's about Captain Frobisher."

Jonathan glanced up and down the lane. There was no one around.

"You best come in," he said.

He directed her into the kitchen where she sat down at the oak table. "Can I offer you a cup of coffee?" Soon a pot of filtered coffee was brewing. Sir Lancelot, as usual, ever on the lookout for a lap to climb on, ensconced himself on hers and she absentmindedly started stroking him.

"Are you from around here. I don't think we've met?" He couldn't help noticing how pretty she looked and hoped that hadn't, and wouldn't, have an effect on his judgement.

"Oh yeah, I live at Bulmer Cottage, you know, in the centre of the village, next to the shop. My dad's Richard Jennings."

The name rang a bell, though Jonathan's head was still fuzzy. He typically didn't wake fully until his first cup of coffee. And then he remembered. He had met him in the Skandlebury Arms. Jonathan also recognized his daughter's name because he'd seen it written before, in the police notes on the Frobisher file. Eleanor Jennings was the witness on the bicycle. It seemed a coincidence she should turn up on his doorstep now.

Jonathan poured out two cups of coffee. "So what can I do for you?" he asked.

"Well, it's a bit awkward," she replied, "I rent a field at the Frobisher's place for my horse. I liked the captain and we got on well. Only as friends," she added hastily. "He shared my love of horses. I never got on with his wife though. I think she was jealous of me. She thought, maybe, that Captain Frobisher and I got on too well, which wasn't true, we were just good friends. He was more like a father to me." She sighed. "My dad is so busy I hardly ever see him. He works up in London and has a very high-powered job. He keeps a flat there and is normally only ever down here at weekends. So I used to ask the captain for advice when I needed it. You know, about relationships and stuff. We would just chat. I really miss him." Her eyes glistened with tears, and she gulped down a mouthful of coffee. "Sorry," she said, "I didn't mean to blurt all that out, but it might explain why I need to find somewhere new for my pony. You see, without the captain I will have to deal with his wife, and I don't want to. So, I was wondering - you have a couple of fields at the back of your house - maybe I could rent them? I will pay a good rent."

Jon smiled again . He liked her lack of guile. "I'd be delighted to let you use my fields. It'll help keep the grass down - they look so untidy at the moment. Actually, I was thinking of buying a couple of goats or something to do the job, but I am sure your pony would be up to the task."

"How much will you charge?"

Jonathan smiled again. "Well, considering your horse will be helping with the grass, how does a big fat zero sound?"

The girl gasped. "Really?"

"Yes, really. You can put your horse there anytime."

"Oh, thank you so much." She was smiling from ear-to-ear.

"The Frobisher's farm is quite a way outside the village. How did you visit your horse?" Jonathan asked, though he suspected he already knew the answer.

"Oh, I cycle there most times," Eleanor replied, "unless I have something heavy to carry, then dad gives me a lift. If he's around," she added.

"I heard police spoke to a witness on a bicycle when the captain died. Was that you?"

"Yes."

"I guess you didn't see anything odd or unusual when you were there?" he said.

"Well no. I groomed my horse in the stable. He's called Captain, by the way. Named after Captain Frobisher, of course." She paused. "It was about ten or so in the morning when I arrived," she continued. "I led him out to pasture. I never saw the captain or his wife. I understand the time of... of his death was around eleven. I left around then. I'd gone to the farm earlier than I normally do as it was the day of the Bellhinton fete. A friend of mine's niece was in the Easter egg hunt and I was helping out there."

"Did you see anyone else on the farm?"

"No, but I did see a white van speed down the drive, passing me. I remembered later that it had red lettering on it. I told the police it was a car. Again her voice faltered, "I wasn't thinking straight. Anyway, they said it was an accident so I didn't tell the police I'd made a mistake. It was probably only a delivery van, but not one I've noticed around here before. Not that that means anything. I'm not interested in cars – or vans for that matter. It could've come from anywhere, I suppose, even as far away as Beckton. Come to think of it, it was driving very fast which struck me as odd. Anyway, why do you want to know all this?" she asked, her small frame stiffening.

Jonathan liked her openness and the way the words kept tumbling out of her mouth. "Can you keep a secret? I've been asked by the police to use my local connections to make a few enquiries into the captain's death. When did you say you saw the white van?"

"It was when I left, so around eleven. I'd just let my horse into the field after grooming him, then I took him for a quick gallop. As I was mounting him, I heard the noise of a vehicle of some sort and turned around and saw the white van. But I don't understand what you mean. Why are you investigating what happened? It was an accident, wasn't it?" Eleanor's pretty face looked anxious.

"Probably," Jonathan said, "but one of the detectives, the one who approached me, isn't so sure. He asked me to find out what I can. He wants me to ask around at Captain Frobisher's cricket club."

Eleanor looked thoughtful for a moment. "You know, come to think of it, there are a few things that puzzle me. The main one being that Captain Frobisher wasn't stupid and would have had to have been pretty dumb to fall out of a hayloft. Also, I went to the farm a couple of days later and looked in the barn. I don't know why. Just curious I suppose. I climbed the ladder to the hayloft. The place was a mess, the hay that was there was all over the place. It could've been because there'd been a struggle, or maybe it had always been messy. I didn't think much of it at the time, but now you mention it, it does seem strange. You know I'd love to know the truth – if he was murdered or not. But why would anyone want to murder him? He was harmless and very popular in the village." Eleanor picked up her empty coffee cup and took it over to the sink. Sir Lancelot landed on the floor with a grunt.

"Can I..." she hesitated for a moment and then said firmly, "Can I help you with your investigation? If it was murder, well, I want justice done for him, Mr. Chambers."

Jonathan laughed. "I'd be delighted if you would join me. I've always wanted an assistant. Although to assist in what I don't know yet… We need to visit the scene of the captain's death and maybe interview the widow; perhaps you could look into the white van - look on the internet for any local businesses with a red logo. And please call me Jon."

"You know," said Eleanor, "if it wasn't for the fact that a man I knew and loved was dead then this could be fun. I've always wanted to be a detective."

"Well, remember, if its murder, it could be dangerous too. A person who has killed once won't hesitate to do it again if they feel threatened."

"I'll be careful," Eleanor said returning from the sink, "I'd best get on. I'll do some research, and then later this afternoon I'll move my horse to your field."

"Will you have stuff to collect too, like saddles and blankets?" asked Jonathan. "You can store it in the shed in the east field. I'll show you where that is and give you a key."

"Oh thanks, you are so nice. I suppose I'll need to ask my dad to help transport the tack." Seeing Jonathan's puzzled look, she smiled, "that is, all the stuff that the horse has when I'm out riding like saddles and reins. There's plenty of room in the back of his Land Rover."

She seemed reluctant to ask her dad for help.

"Don't bother your dad," he said, "I'd be pleased to help you move stuff. We can visit the scene of the supposed crime, and maybe I can interview the widow."

"Oh, thank you that would be great, and we can get the investigation off the ground. How about this afternoon, say four? The horse should be in your field by then."

"Yes, that'll be fine. Tell me," said Jonathan, changing the subject, "do you know Bert the mechanic?"

Eleanor smiled. "Yes, he's nice. He's repaired my bike for me a few times. He never charges me."

"Oh, and do you know DI Sims?" he asked.

"Who?" the girl looked puzzled.

"DI Sims of Beckshire Police."

"Er...no. It was DC Dennis that took my statement. I've never heard of DI Sims. Thanks for the coffee," she said as she turned to leave, "and for letting me graze my horse on your field." Sir Lancelot took the opportunity to go outside, running between her legs and nearly knocking her over.

"Sir Lancelot!" said Jonathan. The cat took no notice but wandered out into the spacious garden to do whatever business he had in mind.

Jonathan followed her into the hall and stood at the doorway and watched her walk down the front path, her tight jodhpurs accentuating her slim legs. He sighed and closed the front door softly before picking up his phone and dialling a number.

"Can I speak to DI Sims?"

"Sorry, we don't have a detective here by that name," replied a female voice.

"Are you sure?"

There was a sigh on the other end and then a rustle as the call handler covered the receiver with her hand. "Phil," she called, her voice muffled, "did a DI Sims ever work here?"

Jonathan couldn't hear the reply but a moment later the woman returned to the line.

"Oh, yes, apparently we did have a DI Sims. He retired several years ago. He's gone to Australia, we believe, to live with his son. Any particular reason you want to know?"

"Oh no," Jonathan said, "his name just cropped up in a conversation." Knowing the excuse to be flimsy, he rapidly replaced the receiver.

As he ruminated on the events of the day he recalled how Eleanor and possibly most of the village were not so confident that the death had been an accident. Jonathan ever sensitive to violent death had begun to feel that if there was any doubt it was his duty to try and find out what really happened. Sheer curiosity was a factor too. Jonathan knew in his heart that the challenge laid down would have to be met and some good might come out of his investigation. And yes, Bert was right, a project would help him focus on other things.

The Frobisher case had been closed too conveniently, the stranger had said. Something about meeting targets or saving money. Maybe this chap, who called himself DI Sims, with his fake ID, was connected or had connections to the police and thought, that the Frobisher case was a convenient case, being so local, for him to get involved in. His connections were such that he was able to obtain the police file. Well, the joke would be on him if he could prove that it was murder. However, he was also aware the police would not be too pleased if he proved them wrong, not to mention the killer. He resolved to act cautiously.

Jonathan sighed. He knew he had to take on this intriguing case. Sims may actually have stumbled on the truth. There were so many unexplained issues. Jonathan let his fancy run wild for a moment. Could Frobisher's wife possibly have a motive to get rid of him? He was much older than she was. Maybe she was having an affair with a younger man. The farm was probably worth at least a million, too. Not an inconsiderable sum to inherit. Then there was the cricket club. Was it in any way connected to his death? And, the police statement had indicated the conversion of the barns was being considered by the Frobishers and if news of the plan had got out then it may have prompted a local with extreme resistance to change to take drastic action. And what about Eleanor? There was such an aura of innocence about her. Either she was an exceptional actress, and the van with the red lettering was a deliberate red herring, or she was genuine. Jonathan always considered himself a good judge of character and decided for the moment to believe her.

And he still couldn't place D.I. Sims. Where had he seen him before?

Chapter Five

Kevin lived with his overweight, chain-smoking mother, Mrs. Charles, on the small council estate on the edge of Skandlebury. Mrs. Charles was mother to a string of boys with different dads. They were jobless and at least one serving time at His Majesty's pleasure. Before the ravaging effects of age, drink, poor diet and smoking had robbed Mrs. Charles of her looks, she had a reputation of being a rather loose but attractive woman, jeeringly known amongst her self-righteous neighbours as the bicycle of Skandlebury.

Kevin was probably the most intelligent and good looking of the Charles brood, but he usually used his saturnine good looks and what intellectual gifts he possessed for malevolent purposes. He was responsible for much of the local petty crime – he had a contempt for private property and a smouldering resentment for anyone more refined or well to do than himself.

He also had a morally corrosive effect on many of the local, generally well brought up, middle class children in the locality. He added excitement to their humdrum lives and several joined him in his criminal activities – mainly petty theft and vandalism. He took girls to the railway embankment, where the line skirted the village to the south. There he plied them with cans of cheap lager, gave them various dubious substances to smoke, and tried to convince them to have sex with him.

Kevin was the bane of all the middle-class parents' lives and most of their offspring were banned from seeing him. Thus, it was not unknown, if you had sharp eyes and were out late, to spot teenagers in the middle of the night dangling out of bedroom windows on their way to an illicit liaison with this one youth crime wave.

Kevin was blamed, quite rightly, for much of the petty crime that took place in the village: thefts from the village store, broken windows, and fights outside the pub on a Saturday night. He had long since been banned from the Puss-in-Boots. Upon being informed of the ban he proceeded to throw bricks through all the windows. No action was taken due to lack of evidence.

There seemed to be little chance of him leaving the village unless it was for a spell in prison. He had disappeared for a peaceful six months last year after being caught stealing lager from the village shop. Villagers assumed he was in a prison or a young offender's institution.

Kevin had one weakness. While most of the girls he hung around with meant nothing to him, other than a chance to have casual sex, he appeared to have developed a strange attraction for one particular girl. Eleanor had rejected his approaches on several occasions, refusing even to speak to him. She made him feel like nothing more than something loathsome that had crawled out from a drain. He did not normally have a problem with self-esteem and could not understand why she continually spurned him.

That morning Kevin was on his way to the village shop to purchase a fresh supply of cigarettes. Just as he was about to enter the shop, he saw Eleanor crossing the green towards School Lane. Abandoning his quest for cigarettes, he followed her, careful to stay out of sight. He saw her go up the lane and turn into a large house on the right. He retreated to the bottom of the lane and waited for her to emerge. Eleanor was in the house for about half an hour. He didn't mind waiting.

As Eleanor returned back down the lane, he sprang out in front of her.

"Hi, Ellie," he said. Eleanor glanced at him and quickened her pace. "In a hurry?"

"Yes," replied Eleanor, "to get away from you. And don't call me Ellie."

"Now, now, no need to be rude. Just want to chat. I've got something important to tell you. How about we sit over there?" He pointed to a wooden bench on the edge of the green.

"Sorry I'm very busy, must dash."

"Oh, go on," wheedled Kevin, "I have something very important to tell. Once I've told you I'll leave you alone."

Eleanor turned to him her pretty face marred by a sneer. "Now why don't I believe you? Is it because everyone knows you're a liar and a thief?"

She quickened her pace. He stood in her path, a look of menace on his face. "You do as I tell you, babe," he said and grabbed her arm.

They were nearly back at the village store.

"Get off me!" Eleanor said, trying to wrench her arm out of Kevin's grip. "There will never be anything between us - ever!"

"You don't get it do you?" snarled Kevin, his grip on her arm tightening as he began dragging her towards a wooden bench on the green. "I just wanna talk - something you'll really wanna know."

"Get away from me!" she repeated more desperately. With a huge effort she finally succeeded in releasing her arm from his grip.

"Just listen to me," said Kevin, "I need…"

He was interrupted by the appearance of a man. He had clearly been gardening as he was carrying a spade and was wearing green wellington boots. His face was red with rage. "You get your filthy hands off my daughter, you scum bag!" he roared.

Kevin retreated. He ran across the green towards the Council estate.

"You ever come near her again and I will flatten your stupid skull with this spade." Kevin raised two fingers and ran faster.

"You OK, darling?"

"Yes, Dad thanks, but I could have handled it myself."

"Well, someone needs to teach that lout a lesson. Where have you been, love?"

"I went to see Jon Chambers about renting his fields for my horse."

"Jon Chambers… that's the guy who lived over at Lower Tiddenham, isn't it. His parents died abroad leaving him the manor. Brought up by an uncle I believe. Must have made a mint, I'd say. Yes, met him at the pub occasionally. I bought him a drink once. I can't believe the cost of a pint these days!" Richard Jennings paused then said: "How much did he charge you, poppet? I imagine it's quite a lot."

"No dad. He's not charging. He thinks the horse will help keep the grass down."

"Oh, right."

"Anyway Dad, I need to go - got things to do."

"Don't you want to rest for a bit? You look a bit shaken."

"No dad. I'll be fine, honest."

By this time they were outside Bulmer Cottage. Eleanor let herself in and her dad continued his digging of the flowerbed at the front of the house.

Inside, Eleanor ran up the stairs and flung herself on her bed, sobbing.

Chapter Six

At 4 pm that afternoon, having recovered from her sobbing fit, Eleanor made her way back to Jon's house. She had tried to analyse why she had been so emotional. Was it her father and the unreasoned, almost murderous, fury he had shown upon the arrival of Kevin? As far as she knew her father hardly knew Kevin. Why was he then so angry? Kevin was being forceful, yes – but in broad daylight? What did her father think – that he would assault her in public? She knew that part of her distress lay in the knowledge that her father had a raging, unreasoning temper. Deep down she knew it was something else, something deeper, something she refused to acknowledge out loud.

BLOOD, SAND, AND CREAM TEAS

As she approached the house she saw a blue van in the drive emblazoned with the name "Skandlebury Carpets". She peeped in at the sitting room window and noted two men hard at work.

She'd found Jonathan in a deckchair in his back garden sipping tea. "Hi Jon," she said brightly. He was shirtless and on seeing her he stood up, and, with an old-fashioned sense of decency, slipped on a bright Hawaiian shirt. Eleanor noted his muscled torso. She hadn't expected him to be so defined. Or the way it made her heart beat faster.

Jonathan returned the greeting. She declined his offer of a cup of tea, and they set off in his Range Rover. On the way Eleanor told him all about the meeting with Kevin and her father's intervention. Jonathan didn't say much in response. He appeared to be lost in thought.

They arrived at the Frobisher's place after a five-minute drive through the idyllic countryside. One minute they had been driving along a country lane between hedges bursting with spring flowers, bluebells, celandines, primroses, violets and jack-by-the-hedge, with intermittent distant views across country of hazy hills; the next they were plunging through cool woodlands, speckled with flashes of dazzling sunlight, clothed in fragile green, carpeted with bluebells and wild garlic.

As they drove up the gravel drive towards the main house, Jonathan said, "Show me where the captain died. Maybe we can find out more if we look at the scene more critically, rather than accepting his death as suicide or an accident."

Eleanor agreed. "Yes, you're right," she said, "we must find out why he died. I don't think he could have committed suicide. I just don't believe it. He had everything to live for – a beautiful wife, a lovely home and the time to pursue what he loved most: his farm and cricket."

The Range Rover continued on its way until Eleanor said "Stop! There it is! See? The first barn we come to. A fairly secluded place, if you ask me. Ideal place to commit murder!"

Don't jump to conclusions, Ellie," said Jonathan, "we must keep an open mind. Sounds as if you've made yours up already."

Eleanor reddened. She realised she had been carried away with enthusiasm, but more importantly, Jon had called her Ellie, and she found it strangely comforting.

The barn was brick built, clad with black creosoted planks until half way up where it gave way to bare brick. At the top to the side was the doorless opening to the hayloft. With its pitched tiled roof Jon thought it would be ideal for conversion into a separate home. He had seen similar ones all over the county.

Resolving to keep an open mind, Eleanor got out of the Range Rover and Jon followed. The large barn doors at the front were half open and they went in. As they did Jon stopped and sniffed.

"That's odd," he said, "I can smell perfume."

Eleanor sniffed too. "You're right. Smells like the stuff the captain's wife wears - expensive and French. Why did she come here?"

"She's still here," came a voice from above them.

A pair of shapely legs in glossy black leggings appeared on the ladder that went up to the hayloft. Virginie Frobisher was wearing a white silk blouse with a floral brooch at her throat. Her shiny black hair hung loose about her shoulders. She had full red lips and large dark brown eyes. Jonathan felt that the photograph he had seen of her in the police file did not do justice to her sultry beauty.

She turned to face them at the bottom of the ladder.

Jonathan held out his hand. "I'm Jon. Friend of Eleanor's. We've come to collect her tack as she is moving her horse to my paddock. We thought we'd visit the site of the captain's tragic death, to pay our respects."

They shook hands. "Virginie Frobisher," she said. "I'm here for the same reason. We were so happy together. I - I haven't been to the barn since the – er – accident and wanted to see the place where Edwin spent his last moments. I need closure you see. It's been a few weeks and I'm finding it hard to cope without him. He had such great plans you know – to convert the barns into holiday lets. He was confident he could make a good business out of it." She spoke excellent English with only a trace of a French accent. There was a quiver in her voice as she added, half to herself: "How could it have been an accident?"

"You're right," said Jon, "you would have to be very stupid, or very drunk, to fall down from the loft."

Virginie said: "But he never drank much. Anyway, it was morning."

"Precisely," said Jonathan, "it wouldn't be an obvious way to commit suicide, either. Besides it is clear that hitting his head on the plough was what killed him, not the height of the fall. He would not try to kill himself by jumping from such a relatively low height. No. Suicide is ridiculous. It is either a very silly accident... or murder."

Virginie looked at him curiously. "You've obviously thought about this."

"Well," said Jon hastily, reluctant to divulge his assignment, "the captain was very respected, particularly in the cricketing world. I've played against him many a time. I can't believe he died just like that."

"You play for the local village team?"

"Skandlebury."

Eleanor spoke for the first time. "I was very fond of the Captain, too. He was like a father to me."

Virginie looked at her sharply, then her face softened. "Yes, he was very much loved and admired. I cannot imagine who would want to harm him."

Jonathan said: "May we look in the loft? Then we'll collect the tack and go."

"Certainly. Do what you want." There was weariness in her

tone. She sighed and added, "I think I will sell this place any way. It is too big for me, and full of memories of Edwin."

"That would be a pity", Eleanor said, "It is such a beautiful place and you have done such a good job in renovating the house."

"I'm proud of what we achieved here. Thank you for honouring my husband. He had such good friends." With that she walked off briskly towards the house.

They clambered up the ladder and looked around the large but low roofed hayloft. There was a mess of hay and Eleanor, who dealt with hay almost every day, immediately noticed there was something unusual about it.

"This isn't hay for horses, Jon," she said, "this is... *packing* straw. Jonathan examined it - it was thin like two- dimensional spaghetti, and much smoother and paler than normal hay.

"You're right," he said. "The Frobishers must have been storing something in here – something delicate enough to warrant the use of special packing material. I wonder what it was and where it is now."

"That's not all," said Eleanor excitedly. "Look over there!"

In a dark corner was a kettle, plugged into an extension lead which trailed through a hole in the floor and presumably connected to the mains electricity in the main barn. The kettle was placed on a corner shelf next to two mugs. Jon examined them – they were dirty.

"So," Eleanor said, her voice rising in excitement, "at least two people have been here."

"And," added Jon, "they've spent a considerable time in this barn on a regular basis – else why bother with the tea and coffee?" The evidence for the latter was held up by Jon – a bowl of tea bags, a small jar of coffee and what appeared to be a jar of herbs.

Jonathan unscrewed the lid and sniffed the jar. "Cardamom. That's weird."

Eleanor said: "Do you think Virginie knows about this? I bet she doesn't. I bet he was meeting in secret here with someone. Maybe dealing in stolen goods!"

"Now, now," said Jon, for the second time feeling the need to put a damper on Eleanor's very quick but, in his view, flawed deductive skills. "You know Edwin better than I do, but I'm sure he wasn't the sort to engage in illegal activities."

"No, you're right," said Eleanor, thinking hard, "how silly of me! But to have a drink with someone means that you're on good terms with them. Maybe he didn't know about the people using this barn. Maybe he stumbled on their secret hideout and paid for it with his life."

"Right," said Jonathan, "there are plenty of scenarios that could apply here. Firstly... Hey wait! Switch on the light!" As Eleanor did he saw the kettle was not perched on a corner shelf but on a fair-sized wooden cupboard, built into the corner of the barn. Jon bent down and opened it. The cupboard was filled with a couple of sleeping bags!

"So, people are staying the night here!" exclaimed Jonathan, "They must be fugitives of some sort. But how could they possibly hide here without the Frobishers knowing?"

"Think about it," said Eleanor. "This barn is unused, and has been for some years. It is the farthest barn away from the main house, being at least two hundred metres, and it's close to the road. The Frobishers would have no cause to visit it once they moved in. Even if they did – would they climb into the hayloft?"

"Unless they were thinking about an alternative use for it – i.e. conversion into holiday homes! I bet on his visit he disturbed the intruders and they shoved him through the loft hatch."

"Looks like it," said Eleanor. "Shall we call the police?"

Jonathan considered for a moment, then said: "We could, but it's just a theory. The evidence of people staying the night doesn't prove anything. Could just be a couple of homeless people. I don't think the police would reopen the investigation on such flimsy evidence. It would also be a considerable loss of face to admit the possibility that they were wrong."

"Homeless people with a liking for tea and coffee - with cardamom?" Eleanor said. "You've got to admit it's odd and the police certainly didn't pick it up. I..."

"Because they thought it was an accident." Jonathan interrupted. "Much better for crime figures not to have an unsolved murder on your books."

"Maybe we're being a bit cynical about the police. They didn't know Edwin like I do. They didn't know he was meticulously careful and would never have accidentally fallen out of a hayloft. Nor would they know, unless they asked, that he was the sanest guy on the planet with everything to live for – a glamorous French wife, plenty of money, and a beautiful, newly renovated, home – he had no reason whatsoever to top himself."

"True," agreed Jon, "yet he was on a run of bad form in his cricket and his club were considering replacing him as an opener with an ex-county man."

"Really!" Eleanor raised her eyebrows, "Hardly grounds for suicide or murder!"

"You'd be surprised," Jonathan said, "many people who are passionate about their hobby would kill to protect it."

"You'd have to be a real psycho to do that! And I don't think Edwin would be suicidal over a loss of form."

"Well, I'll try to find out tomorrow night. We're playing Edwin's old team in a friendly tomorrow, so I could ask around."

Jon was rummaging around in the cupboard again. His fingers closed round something hard and square. He drew it out. It was a framed photograph. He glanced at the photo. He looked again. In an instant he was back in the hot sandy desert of the Middle East.

"What have you got there, Jon?" asked Eleanor. Then seeing his pale, horror-stricken face added anxiously, "Are you OK?"

"No. We're in danger. Let's go!"

"Why? What's that you're holding?"

"No time to explain now." Jon replaced the picture where he had found it. "Let's go! Quick!"

The note of urgency in his voice galvanised Eleanor into action and she sprinted towards the car, Jon following.

"We'll fetch your tack later. We've got to get the hell out of here!"

As they drove down the lane towards Skandlebury, a white van with the inscription 'Valentine Removals' in big red letters flashed past.

"The white van!" exclaimed Eleanor.

Jonathan didn't look surprised.

"Looks like we got out just in time."

Chapter Seven

Eleanor said no more until they arrived at Jonathan's house, named 'Two Trees.' Both the Scots pines which had given the cottage its name had long since blown down, leaving two rather forlorn stumps on either side of the gate.

Jonathan parked his car on the drive, saw the blue van, and groaned. "The carpet fitters are still here. They must be running late. Why don't we go down to the tea shop and have something to eat? I'll explain, then."

Eleanor acquiesced readily as she was hungry and eager to know why Jon felt the urgent need to flee the barn. They walked down School Lane to the village green. On the left-hand side, a few doors down from the Jennings' cottage was a small tea shop which catered for the locals as an alternative meeting place to the Puss-in-Boots.

They found a table by the window. The only other patrons were an elderly couple, clearly walkers as they both wore corduroy trousers and walking boots and were carrying stout wooden walking sticks, with whom they exchanged greetings.

"Hello," said the man, "lovely day."

"Yes, lovely," Eleanor agreed, "are you out walking?"

"Yes," replied the man, smiling at her question, the answer for which was self-evident, "we've come out from London for the day. Are you local?"

"Sort of. My mum's in London, but we have a cottage in the village where I spend most of my time."

"Don't blame you, it's a gorgeous place. We've been to other villages in Beckshire but this village with its castle is the tops."

"Well, welcome," beamed Eleanor, and sensing that Jonathan was seething with impatience and bursting to talk about what had just happened, ended the conversation with: "and enjoy your tea."

Jonathan ushered Eleanor to a table near the window and they made themselves comfortable.

Bessie, the proprietor's daughter, a plump young lady, about the same age as Eleanor, with a freckled face and ginger hair, came over, notepad in hand.

"Hi, Ellie," she said brightly, "Hi, Jon. How are you both?"

"Fine," Ellie said and kissed Bessie on both cheeks. Ellie aware of Jonathan's impatience to be alone with her, added: "and may we have a cream tea for two, please."

Bessie scribbled down the order and scuttled off.

"Now, shoot!" said Eleanor, leaning forward over the table.

Jonathan was quiet for a moment. "I think they're after me again," he muttered, half to himself. "They're getting closer now. They're in the village."

"Who is?" asked Eleanor, anxiously, looking at Jonathan's pale set face.

Jonathan tried to regain his composure. "You know this isn't easy for me," he said, "and although I feel we're becoming friends, I've only known you for a day. Also, I've never shared such personal details about my life with another living soul."

Eleanor looked at him earnestly. The quiet, tall, modest young man she saw in front of her was rapidly gaining a foothold in her affections. "I know," she said, "it must be difficult. But sometimes it is easier to talk to a relative stranger than someone you know. I promise you I won't tell anybody anything you want to keep a secret."

Jonathan smiled. He in return was beginning to like the pretty, impulsive Eleanor who seemed to have an almost childlike trust in him, even though she had only met him a few hours ago.

There was a silence as Jonathan marshalled his thoughts.

"It's difficult to know where to begin," he said, hesitantly.

"Ok," said Eleanor, "how about – who was that guy in the photo?"

"That guy in the photo in the middle is part of an Arab terrorist cell linked to a group whose Arabic name can be translated as 'Kill the Infidels.'" I believe he is the leader. The two men either side of him are his closest associates. They operate in the Middle East committing acts of terror against any country whose policies or affiliations they don't agree with, particularly if they thought the government was too Western leaning. They were responsible for the bombing of a hotel and were linked with that plane hijacking last year. They've assassinated political figures they don't agree with, too. It was him and his mates who murdered my parents."

Eleanor gasped, her blue eyes round and large. "Wow!" she said, the thought of having one's parents murdered being far too huge a concept for her to grasp immediately. "No wonder you were shocked! But how come? I mean you're from a very English family, I should think, and surely ..."

Jon interrupted. "My dad was a diplomat and anti-terrorism expert linked to a British embassy out in the Middle East. He wanted to serve his country and his fascination for the Middle East led him to study the region at university and to become fluent in Arabic. I think what attracted him was the contrast between the vast hot deserts of the region and the tranquility of the English countryside. You may know that we lived in the Manor House at Lower Tiddenham when in the UK, and you can't get much more bucolic than that!"

Eleanor was not sure what 'bucolic' meant but she didn't interrupt.

Jonathan continued: "He was very successful in combatting terrorism and this particular gang lost most of its members through his intelligence work. There were very few operational terrorists left in the group but three of them were Nawaf, whose picture we saw, and his two henchmen who I know as Khalid and Fahad. Intelligence sources think Nawaf is the leader, but no one is sure. I know nothing about him. He disappeared after the murders, and I have no idea whether he's in prison or even if he's still alive."

There was a pause for a moment as Bessie returned and plonked a tray on their table containing a teapot, two large cups and saucers, two large, delicious looking home baked scones, and pots of cream and jam.

"Here, let's dig in - I'm hungry."

As is the Beckshire tradition, they spread the jam first, and then a thick layer of cream on the warm, delicious smelling scones. There was silence as they ate.

Eleanor poured the tea. Her thoughts were far away in that distant, hostile land, half dreading to hear of the horrific events she knew Jon was about to relate. The other couple in the tearoom were absorbed in conversation, oblivious of the drama being enacted at the table by the window. A fly buzzed angrily on the panes of the bay window at which they sat.

Jon took a sip of tea and continued mechanically as if reluctant to visit horrors on this naïve young girl whose sheltered existence meant she had never even been abroad apart from the occasional package holiday to Spain or Greece.

"So you see, Khalid and Fahad, probably led by the mysterious Nawaf, must have been hell bent on revenge. They wanted to wipe out my family completely, even if it meant pursuing us all over the world. This of course was unnecessary. One afternoon, I was ten years old, they just drew up in a 4 by 4 and sprayed us indiscriminately with bullets and drove away laughing. We had just got back from shopping and the entrance gate was still open. They shot the security guard and then entered the courtyard. We were all there: the driver, helping my Mum and Dad with the shopping, and the maid, hanging out the washing. They all died instantly. They must have forgotten about me, or else thought I was dead, because they didn't bother to check if anyone was still alive. Well, the guy who I assumed to be the leader did, as he looked at my mother to whom I was clinging and didn't seem to notice that I was very much alive. Or maybe they thought no one could survive such a hail of bullets. Anyway, one minute we were a happy family, the next minute I was alone. After an age someone from the embassy, who had arrived for a meeting, found me wandering around in shock. There were dead bodies everywhere."

Eleanor's face was white and drawn. Her lower lip quivering, tears filled her eyes. She said nothing but instinctively reached out her hand and clasped Jon's. Jon continued in a low, shaky voice as he relived the events which had so dramatically changed his life.

"After that I was sent back to the UK and stayed with my uncle who lives near Beckton. He managed my parent's will. Their assets, including the sold manor house, went into a trust fund. My uncle has been great. He and my aunt showered me with love and affection, and I had as normal a childhood as possible from then on." Eleanor was now weeping. He had never met such a sensitive girl before and put his other hand in hers.

"Well, that's it really," he continued somewhat awkwardly – he had a rather old-fashioned British dread of naked emotions - "despite my aunt and uncle's efforts, I was traumatised and frequently I have nightmares about it. It made me determined, however, to succeed in life and to honour my parents.

"Vague thoughts of revenge drove me to get a military training: firstly, through the army cadets at school and then in the Army Reserves. I even trained with the Special Forces for a while. I was thinking of a career in the army, but I think my dad would prefer me to get an academic education, so I took a degree at Oxford. My trust fund matured when I was 21 so I travelled round the world for a bit, and then at the ripe old age of 24 I bought my house here in Skandlebury and buried myself in the countryside which my Dad loved so much. And I've been here for the last two years or so – trying to forget."

Eleanor composed herself, wiping her eyes and blowing her nose on the napkin obligingly provided by Bessie.

"So what do you think the terrorists are doing here? It's too much of a coincidence that of all the places to choose from they should come here. Do you think they're after you?"

"Yes, I do. They're the kind who thinks that the job is half done if there are survivors. They must have found out I wasn't dead and decided to finish the job. Although why so many years later... Also, I was debriefed by the intelligence services and I think information on their location I gave helped foil a plot they were working on and resulted in the capture of Fahad. He was sprung from jail by sympathisers and remains at large as far as I know. I think it must have been Fahad and Khalid staying in the barn, probably plotting my death. However, I can't imagine that's the only reason they're here.

"Terrorists wouldn't come all the way to England just to murder a bloke who had crossed them. I'm sure they're planning a terrorist action as well. After all, little old me is not worth the effort of all that planning and the risks they would have to take. Yes, the more I think about it the more I'm sure that I'm just a small distraction. They're hatching something far bigger. It ties in with what my uncle told me, that the terrorists known as OAK are in England and have regrouped. Recently, too, I read that police in London found a bomb making factory linked to them. I'm not sure that we need to look any further for our murderers. We were right: I expect Captain Frobisher stumbled on the men and was silenced by them. It all fits in."

"What are we going to do?"

"We? I need to decide what to do but I can't get you involved. I'd never forgive myself if anything happened to you. I think I'll stop investigating Captain Frobisher's death and I won't need you as a partner - after all it's obvious who killed him. I'll use the skills I picked up in the TA to survive any assassination attempt. Please for your own safety and my peace of mind we can't be too close. If they think we're an item, then you too are in grave danger. They may capture you just to get back at me and I dread to think what they'd do to you. These sorts of men have a very low opinion of Western girls."

Eleanor nodded. "Well, we are just friends, aren't we? We've known each other for just eight hours." There was an edge to her voice.

"It'll all be over soon, and then...." Jonathan didn't know how to finish the sentence. Eleanor looked at him closely for a moment then leaned over and kissed him on the lips. "Let's go," she said.

Jonathan paid the bill and they left – she returned to Bulmer

Cottage and he went back to his house, the sweet taste of her kiss still on his lips.

Chapter Eight

Gone was the soft breeze, the sunshine, and fluffy clouds. Saturday dawned cold and wet. Rain, mingled with sleet, pounded down, driven by a vicious north east wind.

There was no chance of a cricket match that morning as Jon braved the elements for his early morning run. He pounded through icy puddles, shivering in the cold gale, soaked to the skin. Indeed, he had had a phone call from the club secretary, Claire, the vicar's daughter, saying that the friendly would be postponed to next Saturday and the first League match would be the Sunday of the following weekend.

Jonathan was punishing himself. He wished he hadn't warned

Eleanor to keep away from him. He already missed those blue eyes, glistening with tears of sympathy as he had poured out his life story. Sharing such a deeply personal experience had brought them both closer. They had not yet even had a date but their attraction for each other was palpable. And now he had pushed her away. Was it fear of commitment as well as a desire to protect her? Was he being selfish in wanting to see her knowing that association with him, a marked man, could endanger her life? All he knew was that he desperately wanted to see her again and didn't like the way he had left her without agreeing a future date even if it was just part of a social event. He could have invited her to the cricket social in the pavilion next Saturday. They could just turn up and chat as friends. Anything to relieve that ache of longing.

He found himself running past her cottage: a diversion from his normal route. The curtains were tightly drawn, and he thought ruefully that they were a symbol of the barrier between them. He was convinced that any separation would make Eleanor lose interest in him. The Frobisher investigation had been an opportunity to be together and now that appeared solved, he had lost any reason for contacting her. He ran, on and on, down the road to Beckton and into the woods. He ran further than he usually did and by the time he had got home he was exhausted.

He showered and changed and, feeling at a loose end, wandered down to the village to buy some food and other supplies.

Jonathan was the first customer in the Puss-in-Boots that morning.

******

The week went by slowly without any sign of Eleanor until Wednesday morning when they met in the village shop. Jon was buying milk; Eleanor, cheese, and they met by the refrigerator. A somewhat awkward conversation ensued.

"Hello, Eleanor" said Jon.

Eleanor said "Oh. Hi," in an over bright fashion and proceeded to select some Camembert. Jonathan picked up his milk and took a chance.

"Hey would you like to come to the pub this evening?"

Eleanor looked at him, curious. "I suppose so... but doesn't this mean that I will be getting – how did you put it? – too close to you?"

"Well, you'd be part of our pub quiz team so it would be a non-threatening environment."

No sooner had he said these words than he instantly regretted them. Ellie's bright blue eyes seemed to become icy cold.

"Threatening to whom?"

"Sorry," Jonathan mumbled, "bad choice of words. But you know what I mean. We mustn't let the terrorists think we're an item or they'll get at me by using you as a bargaining chip. I know these men and there is no horror they'll not do if they think it'll further their cause. I just want to protect you that's all."

Eleanor softened. "Okay," she said, "I do like a good quiz. "Let's hope there's a good literature round."

"That's great," said Jonathan, not bothering to hide his enthusiasm. "I'll meet you at the pub about eight. The vicar'll be pleased I've found a replacement for him."

"Who else will be there?"

"Well, there's Claire – she's great at science and nature – and Mike Jones. You know Mike don't you? He's pretty good at most subjects."

"Oh, yes," said Eleanor, much more brightly, "I know Mike and I'm very friendly with Ruth. We sometimes go to church together."

Jonathan was relieved. Her quiz expertise was irrelevant. This was unusual because the local quiz league was as fiercely competitive as the cricket league.

Eleanor arrived at the pub that evening on the dot of eight, the agreed time of their rendezvous. She was casually dressed in jeans and a pink jumper. Jonathan thought she looked stunning but restricted his greeting to a chaste peck on the cheek.

Mike Jones was hilarious company, and Claire was very entertaining; the evening passed by happily enough. Jon felt any awkwardness between him and Ellie slipping away and in a quiet moment – Mike had gone to the bar for more drinks, and Claire to powder her nose – they managed a private conversation.

"Has anything happened since Friday?" she asked. She sounded anxious. "Any sign of the terrorists?"

Jonathan shook his head. "No developments at all. Early days yet, though." he paused for a moment and then added: "Maybe we could see more of each other - as friends." He paused for a moment, then: "Trust me," he continued, "if anything happens that puts you in danger, I'll disappear, and you can pretend we never met."

"You know, I don't mind what dangers we face," Eleanor said as long as we face them together, as friends. Remember I'm your detective partner."

"But we've nothing left to detect. We know what happened to Captain Frobisher."

"We think we know," insisted Eleanor. "But what about the mysterious white van we saw - where did that come from? Who are Valentine's Removals? Where do the terrorists live? Surely if they live in the village someone will know them."

"Depends: they probably keep a very low profile."

"Should we go to the police?"

"Not sure they'll believe us. We could try but not yet. Anyway, they're convinced Nigel's death was an accident and saying he was murdered by terrorists living in a barn sounds a bit far-fetched. They'll probably resent us interfering in a police matter."

Jon saw Claire coming back to the table.

"Hey," he said quickly, "Why don't we meet up tomorrow?

We could throw caution to the wind, look around the castle and have another cream tea."

"That sounds fun. I've only been to the castle once, and I don't know much about it."

"I know it really well - studied the place at school for my local history class, both the castle and the abbey ruins, and as part of my degree thesis. You'll get a very learned guide."

"You studied history?" said Eleanor, somewhat incredulous. She didn't associate her cricket-loving friend with something as academic as history.

"Yes. Scraped through it at Oxford. I nearly wasted a great opportunity to study at such a world-renowned university thanks to partying too much – and cricket!"

Claire rejoined them and Mike came over, bearing a tray of drinks.

"I'll call on you tomorrow, Eleanor," said Jonathan, "I think the weather's clearing up. That's if you're free of course."

"Got nothing on all day."

"Wow," said Jonathan, his eyes widening dramatically.

He got a friendly slap on his arm. Eleanor giggled and said "you know what I mean, silly." Jonathan couldn't help noticing Claire's wry smile.

Eleanor then added: "Claire, why don't you come too? You're always saying you never go and see the castle."

******

The castle tower was a dramatic sight, towering up from the mound, or motte, and Eleanor shivered, imagining the horror the prisoners faced as they were dragged down the steps to the dungeons beneath, now signposted for modern eyes in bright white lettering on a black background.

"You see," Jonathan said, "the Normans wanted to exert their authority on Saxon England so they built these castle keeps, initially in wood, to dominate the surrounding countryside and filled them with knights ready at a moment's notice to deal with any insurrection. Around it would be a wooden fence, or bailey, which would enclose land for horses to graze etc. These forts could be put up quickly and indeed it is believed that the Normans predated a well-known Swedish company in that they brought flat packed castles over with them from Normandy. The villagers would be forced to create the motte as cheap labour and to show who was boss."

Claire yawned. She did not want a history lesson. History did not interest her, but as she noted, Eleanor hung on his every word. "You would make an excellent tour guide," she exclaimed.

Jonathan continued with his speech, explaining the history of the castle right up to the time it was besieged in the English Civil War and partially destroyed.

Claire wandered off and the two were left alone for a while. They sat down on a low piece of the ruined curtain wall, the sun now shining. The wind, in a less hostile direction, was now a gentle breeze.

Eleanor said: "This is fun. We must do this more often. You know when you live in a place you should get to know it. I've been here since a child and only visited this place once and never the ruined abbey. I know nothing about the old church."

"Well, let's go see these places," said Jonathan, "although I don't imagine Claire would come."

"We'll ask Bessie," said Eleanor, "she's always game for new stuff, despite what you may think."

Jonathan liked Bessie but could not imagine that she would be interested in history. Her conversation usually centred on food, popular music and boys.

"We'll give it a shot," he said, half hoping she would say no, and he could give her the tour alone.

Their visit to the castle complete, they found Claire and headed for the tea shop. Bessie was taking a break enjoying a moment in the sun. On seeing their approach, she hastily smoothed down her apron, looking guilty as if she had neglected her work. At the same moment, unseen by the three friends, Kevin walked across the green in the direction of the Beckton Road and his house.

"Hi," said Bessie, brightly, "what can I get for you today?"

The three ordered cream teas, and they were soon sipping tea out of intricately patterned bone china cups and spreading jam and cream lavishly on the scones, still warm from the oven. Jonathan fell into a reverie contrasting in his mind the polite

English traditions with the Middle East where he had lived; the blinding heat of the sun, the swirling dust and the endless desert on the one hand, this green watery corner of England on the other, where the sun peeped cautiously in through the well cleaned window panes, and half drawn flowery curtains.

Bessie and Claire chatted inconsequentially, and Eleanor watched Jonathan in his deep reverie. Bessie left them to their tea.

"A penny for your thoughts, Jonathan," laughed Claire.

"Er... er... What?"

"You were looking rather serious, Jon."

"Oh, you know, just thinking about this and that," said Jon.

"And who would *she* be?"

He laughed. "Not a she. Thinking about how lovely and safe this place is compared to where I used to live. Middle East you know. Still, I suppose there are some benefits." Jonathan remembered the huge full moons that rose over the desert, the many coloured sandstone hills and the warm blue sea where fish darted through pristine coral reefs.

Claire looked interested and was about to quiz him further on this new piece of information about his past when she noticed that Jonathan had put up the shutters again and was back in his reverie.

******

The rest of the week was spent in a similar fashion. Eleanor and Jonathan visited the church and the abbey, accompanied by Bessie.

Bessie seemed more bubbly than usual, and Eleanor got the impression she was concealing big news. Eleanor was unusually sensitive to matters of love at that time and was convinced Bessie was in love, but with whom? There were not very many single lads in the village who were dating material. Kevin? No, he was a lowlife. Billy the son of the publican? He was too immature. Her thoughts ranged over other single young men and concluded that she must have been mistaken unless somehow the stay-at-home Bess had been mingling with male talent from neighbouring villages, or even Beckton. But what about Jonathan? She could see that he got on well with her. He had enthusiastically pointed out the 17th Century oak box to Bess that used to contain church records and the oldest stained glass dating back to the 15th century and explained the story from the Book of Revelation which was behind the most spectacular window showing Michael slaying the dragon. Before now, Bess had never displayed the slightest interest in local history but now she seemed to be lapping it up. Jonathan was a good teacher but was that enough to explain her sudden enthusiasm for the past? Eleanor realised she was probably being a little paranoid and decided to keep her suspicious thoughts in check.

Bessie of course had to work most of the week, as did Claire. But they were never alone. They took Mike Jones and his wife

Ruth's rather lively twin boys out for a walk by the river Beck where they paddled in the cool water and caught minnows with fishing nets. As they got to know each other more, both felt an enormous irresistible attraction building.

Chapter Nine

The next day was Saturday, the day of the rescheduled friendly with Bellhinton. Eleanor decided to go for a walk. Unlike most of the village, she wanted to avoid the match. This was partly because she had no interest in cricket, and partly because she felt she could no longer see Jonathan as just a friend. As far as she was concerned, they should either start dating or never see each other again. Eleanor was still in turmoil over their conversation in the teashop a week ago and wanted to put some distance between herself and the village. Above all she wanted to be alone. She felt she was falling for Jonathan but was worried about Bess. Did she have feelings for him? She seemed unusually interested in history and that was very out of character. They also seemed to get on very well. Should she confront her friend?

And was Jonathan genuine when he said that a close relationship could be dangerous? Or was he simply frightened of commitment? She had believed he was splitting them apart purely for her own safety, but the sleepless nights of the previous week had been a fertile seedbed for doubts to grow.

Eleanor took the footpath by the side of the cottages and followed it through a large grassy field. The Norman keep they had visited only a few days ago soared up into the beautiful blue sky. The bitter cold winds, the heavy rain and sleet seemed but a distant memory. It was now a hot day, the gentle southerly breeze bringing with it the sweet scents of spring. Eleanor wore long leather riding boots over her jeans as it was still muddy underfoot. She had a rucksack on her back containing some food and a towel. She had planned a dip in the cold stream, as she always found this soothing, so was wearing a swimming costume under her clothes.

The path took her through a beech wood, clad in fresh spring green. Mud squelching underfoot, she enjoyed the mist of bluebells stretching out on either side. More fields followed and then she heard the sound she loved: the Skandle brook bubbling over gravel as it made its way to the village from the foot of the chalk hills a few miles away. She followed the brook for a mile or so, reveling in the sunshine and the peace of the countryside.

Eleanor found her favourite place by the brook, where it was deepest, fringed with reeds and yellow iris. A natural pool had formed. It looked cool and inviting. She swung the rucksack off her back and took out her picnic rug which she spread on the ground. She quickly undressed and, closing her eyes, took a deep breath and dived into the shallow water. She gasped as the cold water struck her like an oncoming train. A family of moorhens scuttled to safety, clucking in alarm. Soon she was swimming vigorously, enjoying the delicious coolness of the water. She swam from bank to bank and then lay on her back and floated, enjoying the warm sun on her skin.

When she eventually began to feel chilly, she scrambled out and towelled herself dry. She lay down in the sun and, once more, warmth crept into her body. She stretched out on the luxurious rug and closed her eyes, exhausted after so many restless nights. She was soon lulled into a deep sleep by the sound of the brook, the birdsong and the warm sun on her body.

******

In the meantime, Jonathan had prepared for the cricket match and, dressed in his whites, his trusty bat in hand, had entered the cricket pavilion for a preseason briefing.

Arthur Murray, the outgoing captain was chairing the meeting. Sitting next to him was the man Jonathan knew as DI Sims.

Arthur clapped his hands and the team fell silent: "Good morning everyone. As you know I'm retiring and Mike was to take my place. However, at a hastily convened meeting a fortnight ago, which quite a few of you were unfortunately unable to attend, we decided to appoint a new captain. Mike has been having doubts recently as to whether captaincy was really his thing. So, may I introduce our new captain, recently settled in the village – Nawaf al Hamdi? He approached me wanting to join the team and demonstrated to a few of us that he is an excellent all-rounder. He was vice-captain of his university cricket team and has excellent credentials. It makes me hopeful that we will have a great season...."

At this point Jonathan stopped listening and stared at the new captain in horror. So that was who Sims had reminded him of. His mind flew back to that scene in the desert. Those wide staring eyes boring into him as he clung to his dead mother.

Without further thought Jonathan got up. "Sorry... I've got to go," he muttered as he left.

In a daze Jonathan climbed in to his car and sat there for a moment. Fear and blind panic overcame him as he sat motionless trying to process this shocking development. It didn't seem real. Why wasn't the man in jail? If not, surely, he would be known to the authorities who would, at the very least, be monitoring his activities as a known OAK member and possibly their leader. Thoughts were racing through his head. He would have to resign from the club. He would leave Skandlebury. He would have to expose Nawaf to the club and the police. He couldn't be left unhindered to carry out a possible terrorist attack, or murder him.

He needed to talk and wondered if Eleanor was home.

While Eleanor was busy settling down by the riverbank, Jonathan was knocking on her door. He waited patiently but there was no reply. *Maybe she's gone to the Frobisher farm*, he thought, but no, her bicycle was propped up on the side wall to the cottage. He looked across the village green, shading his eyes from the bright sun. Not a single person was in sight. He soon ascertained that she was not in the village shop or tearoom. He didn't bother to check the pub as he had never seen her in there before on her own and the last time she had been there was for the quiz.

As Jonathan reluctantly made his way back to the cricket field car park, he noticed just to the side of her cottage a patch of mud with fresh boot prints in it. They were quite dainty prints, certainly not Wellington boots. Maybe they were Eleanor's. He decided to followed the path. If it didn't lead to Eleanor, at least it was a nice day for a walk and it would give him time to process the events of the morning.

As Jonathan was striding over the fields, Eleanor had just drifted off to sleep.

He arrived at the brook and spotted Eleanor asleep on the rug.

"Ellie!" he called, "Ellie!" The girl stirred in her sleep. Jonathan called again and she was suddenly wide awake and sitting up looking around her in alarm.

"Ellie, it's me, Jon!"

"Oh, hi Jon!" She gave a sigh of relief. "What are you doing here? I thought you were at the cricket match."

"Yes, I was, but something awful's happened."

"Look," she said, "let me get dressed and we'll talk."

She disappeared behind a hawthorn bush and emerged a few moments later, fully dressed.

"What's happened."

Jonathan told her everything.

"Don't do anything rash, Jon." Eleanor said. "Running away may not be a good thing. It's probably better to stay in the village, in a community, rather than make a run for it. And anyway, wherever you go you could put other people in danger. Stay here, stay in the club. You won't be playing for a week so you won't have to play under his captaincy. Maybe we could talk to the club and the police but not right away. Who knows, the police might be on to him. We don't know yet."

The warm sun shone down from the clear blue sky. Around them a bee buzzed before settling on the pink and white blossom of a hawthorn bush.

"Let's stay here for a bit and you can share my picnic. We're safe here."

Jonathan assented, though he didn't feel hungry and sat down next to Eleanor.

He slowly ate the sandwich she had passed him.

They said very little but Jonathan felt the peace of that riverside spot sink into him and watched the family of moorhens swimming happily once again.

It was a much calmer Jonathan that finally stood up and said "OK, shall we go?"

He helped her pack and they set off for Skandlebury.

"Try not to worry," Eleanor said as they hiked across a grassy meadow bright with celandine, primrose and cowslip. "I'll support you all the way, even if we must not be too close."

Jonathan felt a surge of affection for Eleanor and kissed her on the cheek. She turned to him and gave him a hug. Her arms wrapped around him and he knew he never wanted her to let go.

Above them a skylark sang as it started its upward flight and Jonathan followed its flight until it became a tiny, almost invisible speck, in the cerulean sky.

"'He rises and begins to round; He drops the silver chain of sound,'" Eleanor whispered. The lark vanished from sight lost in the vastness of the sky, but its 'silver chain of sound' tinkled down to them. Somehow present dangers seemed less real as they walked on, hand-in-hand.

They crossed through the bluebell woods, rabbits scuttling into the nettles at its edge, and soon they were back in the village.

"Come in for a coffee," said Eleanor.

"Thanks. Where's your dad?"

"Probably at the match. He'll be at the village hall do tonight. Never misses a chance for a drink. We'll be alone here, my sister's at Mum's in London. Mum's a lawyer and very busy just like Dad," she added a little bitterly. "Oh, I'm so sorry I didn't mean to complain about my folks, especially as you…"

Before she could finish her sentence, Jonathan kissed her gently on the mouth. She closed her eyes, wrapped her arms around his neck and kissed him back. It was everything she wanted. Jonathan pulled back. "I'm sorry," he said, "I didn't mean to"

"Don't be." Eleanor said, resting her head against his chest, "I've been waiting for you to do that for ages."

"Maybe we should get some coffee now," Jonathan said.

They sat down for coffee. Jonathan said: "You know I think we should go to the cricket do tonight. We can go separately. I can keep tabs on Nawaf and maybe we can double check if anyone knows anything about Captain Frobisher's death. Despite all we've been through I would like to know for certain that it was Nawaf's sidekicks that killed him. Somehow it doesn't seem to add up. Also, as you said, it would be safer to carry on as normal. Besides nothing could happen. The whole village will be there."

Eleanor assented. Everything in her wanted to go with Jonathan, but she recognized the good sense of keeping apart. Hopefully soon they wouldn't have to hide their love away.

Chapter Ten

The bar in the cricket pavilion was tastefully decorated in pastel shades of blue. Tables were scattered around the room each seating four people; squashy sofas and armchairs were also provided for more relaxed social interaction. The walls were covered with cricketing memorabilia – framed photographs of presentations, a rogue's gallery of former cricket captains (Jonathan noticed that this year's future captain had not yet been added), and glass-fronted cupboards, filled with silver trophies. A couple of signed cricket bats from county teams also adorned the walls, their handles crossing, and dotted here and there were cricket-themed paintings by a talented local artist.

That night the cricket club's social committee had laid on a buffet to celebrate the new season and to host their guests, Bellhinton. The local villagers had also been invited.

It was a chance for the ladies of the village to dress up and Eleanor did not disappoint in a clingy black evening dress with a slit up the side. Jonathan could not keep his eyes off her.

The only hostile eyes on Eleanor were those of Mrs. Charles who had waddled in early to be the first to graze at the buffet. She was tucking into a plate of sausage rolls and slices of pork pie with gusto, but there was no doubt the gaze directed at Eleanor was suspicious and unfriendly.

The first drinks were free, and Jonathan was soon nursing a pint of the local ale, deep in conversation with Mike Jones, whilst Eleanor, glass of white wine in hand, walked over to where Bessie was standing alone. Maybe she could tease out of her friend a little more information on her love life. Out of duty to their dormant detective partnership she also wanted to find out more about what had happened at the fete.

"Hi, Bess," she said.

"Oh hi, how are things?"

"Fine, thanks. What have you been up to, since I saw you yesterday?"

"Oh, we've been very busy at the café today. We had two coach loads of tourists in for lunch. The tourist season has begun. Must be the fine weather after all the rain we've had."

"Well," smiled Eleanor, "now you're an expert on local landmarks you could be their tour guide."

Bess laughed and said, "Yes. Jon's a great historian, and he can definitely make the subject interesting. I never liked history at school, probably because we had that awful Mr. Bottomley. He used to fall asleep in his own lessons. They were so boring…"

"Yes, weren't they?" said Eleanor who had been Bess's classmate at Beckton High School. "Do you remember when the boys who had collected dead wasps opened a jar full of their rotting corpses?"

"That was funny," giggled Bessie. "The smell was so bad we had to leave the classroom and continue the lesson in the library."

"We were bad. We used to deliberately leave our half-eaten sandwiches and apple cores around to attract mice and rats."

"Oh, and one lesson he was talking about the Black Death being a plague carried by rats and what should scuttle across the classroom? Anyway, I'm glad Jon made the past come to life, unlike dear old Bottomley."

"Yes, I can genuinely say that Jon has roused in me an interest in history."

"Was that all he aroused in you?" Eleanor asked.

"Oh no, nothing like that," said Bessie hastily, "I'm actually dating someone else, but he swore me to secrecy. Not sure why. Hey, what about you and Jon?"

Eleanor blushed and laughed, relieved. "Hmm, let's just say

things are developing." Eleanor couldn't think of the right word to encapsulate the start of their relationship.

"Well good luck with him. He's a great guy."

"And you too, with your mysterious friend."

They chatted inconsequentially for a while and then Eleanor said: "I expect you were at the village fete at Bellhinton a few weeks ago."

"Yes, we were. We had a stall there selling cakes and coffee. We did really well. One guy ate four slices of our cherry cake. Couldn't get enough of it."

"Did you notice anyone missing from the fete that would normally be there?"

"Why do you want to know?"

Eleanor debated within herself whether to tell the real reason why she had asked and then decided it could do no harm.

"Well, you know Captain Frobisher died that day. We don't think it was an accident or suicide: we think it was murder".

Bessie gasped, her eyes wide. "Really?" She sighed. "He was such a nice man. He came into the teashop regularly, sometimes with his wife, sometimes just him. He always gave me a generous tip. I can't imagine anyone wanting to kill him. Have you told the police?"

"Not yet. We don't have much evidence. Just a hunch really."

"But who do you think did it?"

"We're not sure but think it must be someone local," Eleanor said. "So did you notice anyone missing at the fete? Or anything unusual?"

"Only Kevin. He was there early. Picked a fight with a stall owner and left in a hurry, chased by the stewards. But you mustn't blame Kevin for everything bad," she added.

Bessie's eyes glazed over as a memory came flooding back. It was midsummer last year. The night was hot. Kevin had come into the café and asked her out. This had not been the first time they had gone out, but somehow, she felt that tonight would be special. After she had finished work, they had wandered around the village. She remembered Kevin almost shyly grabbing hold of her hand and the tingly sensation his touch made. They eventually had made their way to the railway line that ran a few hundred metres behind the Puss-in-Boots; Kevin having her hand in one hand and a six pack of beer in the other. Once on the embankment they had begun kissing. She had felt Kevin's surprisingly muscular body pressed against hers and his breath smelled of peppermint. She was wearing rather tight tiny shorts and she felt deliciously vulnerable. Kevin, breathing heavily, began to unbutton her blouse and then turned his attention to her shorts. She felt them slipping down her legs. Her flimsy silk knickers, totally unsuitable as a barrier between her chastity and a lusty male, followed. She recalled lying on her back in the fragrant summer grass, gazing up at a full harvest moon, the lager she had drunk making her feel relaxed and giggly. He had been surprisingly tender, aware that it was her first time. Kevin turned out to be a very experienced love maker. She felt it had been the single most pleasurable moment of her life and had been bitterly disappointed that over the next few weeks their relationship had petered out inexplicably. Until recently...

"Bessie, Bessie, are you OK?"

Eleanor's concerned voice snapped her back to the present.

"Oh, er, yes. What was I saying?"

"You were telling me about Kevin picking a fight with one of the stallholders. I was asking you if there was anyone you had noticed missing from the Easter Fete."

"Oh, that's right. Let's see. Your dad for a start. He usually turns up to these things. I think he likes to feel that he belongs in the village. Actually, lots of people who would normally be there were missing. Some stayed for the first hour and left. Others didn't turn up at all."

"Did you notice anything odd in anyone's manner? I was busy helping with the Easter egg hunt, so I missed most of it.".

"Well, Cathy Winter nearly cried when she came second in the cake competition, after winning for the past six years. She made that nice cherry cake for us, and, oh yes, your dad did turn up right at the end. I remember because Kevin was with him, and they were deep in conversation. Then your dad walked off in one direction and Kevin in the other. That was all I saw of him."

Eleanor looked shocked. Only yesterday they seemed to be the worst of enemies and yet just four weeks ago, they were talking to each other. What was going on?

"Did my dad seem shocked or angry or anything?"

"It was difficult to tell. They were too far away, and my stall was pretty busy. We had discounted the cakes that hadn't sold and there was a queue."

"Jonathan, wasn't there either, as far as I know," she added, "in fact when I think about it, the fete wasn't anywhere near as well attended as last year."

They walked over to the buffet and filled paper plates with food. The room was beginning to fill up, a queue forming at the buffet. Bess got her food first and was soon deep in conversation with a young cricketer from Bellhinton.

Eleanor refilled her glass with white wine, extricated herself from a clumsy chat-up attempt by Billy Landsman, the lanky son of the landlord of the Puss in Boots, and went off to look for Jonathan.

Jonathan was propping up the bar, still talking to Mike Jones.

"I was chatting to the vicar," Mike said, slurring his words, as he launched into a drunken monologue. "He loves talking to me by the way. I think intellectual conversations are a bit lacking around here. Anyway, he mentioned how few people there were of other religions or none around here, and I said that our new captain was from the Middle East and had rented a cottage down Hangman's Lane. I also saw him in the shop with two friends of Middle Eastern appearance and wondered if they could play cricket as well as Nawaf. The vicar said how delighted he would be to welcome our Muslim friends to the village, although of course we shouldn't assume that that is their religion. It was great, he said, that the village at last was embracing diversity. I think they all live together in the same house. Edna said she saw them, on the morning of the fete, leave their cottage, The Willows, I think."

Edna Perry was a sharp-eyed, sharp-tongued woman in her 40s who rarely missed anything that went on in the village.

"Hi darling," said Eleanor, approaching and kissing Jonathan on the cheek.

"Oh, are you two together?" said Mike, "Congratulations."

Eleanor gave Mike a hug. "Thanks," she said, "how's Mrs. Jones?"

"She's fine. Got her hands full with the twins. She's started helping out at the school too, as a dinner lady."

"As if she hasn't got enough to do!"

"Money," sighed Mike Jones, "you won't believe how much my twins cost!"

The evening passed quickly enough. Jon chatted to the Bellhinton cricketers and was introduced to Alan Hardy. He had acquitted himself well at the cricket match....

Alan Hardy, a short stocky dark-haired man, professed sorrow at Frobisher's death and said so. He didn't think it could be suicide because although he was being eased out of the club there were no hard feelings. In fact, Edwin had said that he wished him well. He was upset at his lack of form, though, saying he was getting twinges in his back, but seemed resigned to the fact that his cricketing days would soon be over.

The only other person Jon spoke to was Charlie Melville, Bellhinton's wicket keeper. He was also a farmhand at the Frobisher farm.

"Where were you at the time of the captain's death?" he asked.

Charlie scratched his head as if trying to summon up coherent thought. He had been enthusiastically downing the pints since his arrival. He had a ruddy weather-beaten face, tangled brown hair and washed-out blue eyes. He spoke with a Beckshire burr and had attempted to smarten himself up by donning an ancient tweed suit and a thin knitted tie.

Charlie's answer came slowly, and with a lot more head scratching.

"Now let me see... That would be the day of the Easter fete, wouldn't it? I left my cottage at about ten that morning. It was my day off, you see. I had been asked to help at the fete. My job was mainly shifting tables, setting up stalls and such. Oh, and I helped finalise the show jumping course. I believe young Eleanor Jennings on Captain won it for the second year running."

Jon couldn't help feel a glow of pride for his new girlfriend's achievements, but was not to be diverted.

"So, did you see anyone leave or enter the farm? After all, your cottage is further down the lane so you must have passed the entrance to Pollards Farm."

"No... Oh, only Eleanor. She was cycling up the drive to the farm. Gone to tend to her horse I expect. But why are you asking these questions? You haven't joined the police, have you?"

"Oh no," replied Jonathan, hastily, "Eleanor and I are not sure that his death was an accident and we want to find out the truth."

Charlie rubbed his chin thoughtfully. "You may be right there. He was a very careful man and I can't see him falling through a hayloft by accident. He wasn't suicidal either. He was a positive guy and had loads to look forward to. He was really good to me, too, taking me on after the old owners left and letting me stay on in the cottage. I don't get on so well with his missus now. She orders me around and is always criticizing my work." He paused, then added: "She doesn't seem that sorry he's dead either."

Jonathan was surprised at this. She had seemed distraught when they had met at the barn. Was she acting or had Charlie got it wrong?

He decided not to comment.

"So," said Jonathan, "did you see anyone else apart from Ellie enter or leave the farm as you drove past?"

"Nope," replied Charlie emphatically, "not a soul, except as I've already said, Eleanor. She had just turned up the drive when I passed her."

"You didn't see a white van with red lettering on it?"

"Nope," said Charlie again.

Jonathan recalled that the van had been seen by Eleanor as she had left the farm about the time of the murder and had disappeared down the lane long after Charlie had driven past in his battered old Skoda.

"Anyway," said Charlie, "nice talking to you. Hope you find out the truth as to how he died." With that he wandered off to chat with some of his Bellhinton cricket friends.

Skandlebury's new captain arrived half an hour later. He ignored Jonathan all evening. This in itself spoke volumes. After all he was opening the batting with him, and it would be perfectly normal for a new captain to try to get to know his key players in a social context. Jonathan still couldn't decide whether to resign from the club but, as the next game was a week away, he didn't need to do anything hasty. The outgoing captain had accepted his garbled apology for deserting his club at their first match of the season, so his position was secure. And who was it that said keep your friends close, but keep your enemies closer?

Eleanor's father arrived soon after Mrs. Charles had ensured that there was no food left. He turned angrily to the offending woman who stared at him, her mouth unashamedly full of ham and tomato sandwich. He collected a pint of beer from the bar, and Eleanor joined him.

"Hi, Dad."

"Hi, darling, how are you doing? You were in bed when I left for the cricket match. What have you been up to all day?"

"Oh, this and that," said Eleanor listlessly. She seemed to find it harder and harder to talk to her dad. "I went for a walk."

"Seen any more of Kevin?"

"No," she said.

"Good. He's utter scum!"

"Why do you hate him?" she asked.

Her dad did not reply and Eleanor continued: "You were seen talking to Kevin at the Easter fete. Just what is your relationship with him? You hate him yet you also socialize with him? I didn't think you knew him personally. How come you know him more than you let on? You're holding something back from me aren't you, dad?"

"Well... yes, er, two weeks ago I talked to him casually," he blustered, evading her questions.

Eleanor remained silent. That was not the impression she got from Bess.

"Anyway, not much of a do tonight, eh? Especially as that wretched woman has eaten all the food. She's a human vacuum. Still, at least I got a free beer."

"That's not entirely fair, Dad; you've only just arrived. Of course, all the food is gone."

Richard glared at his daughter as if he expected more support from her, and then said, "Well, must be moving on. Got people to see. See you later." And with that he was off, leaving Eleanor marvelling at how distant their relationship had become.

The night was cool and clear, as Jon and Eleanor left the pavilion just before midnight and walked to the village green where Jon had parked his Range Rover.

As they were walked, they swapped notes on what they had gleaned from their conversations; the news that the enemy were living in Hangman's Lane, that the relationship between Kevin and her dad had apparently not always been so hostile, and the long list of absences from the fete which meant that it was useless to try and deduce anything from the absence or presence of villagers. Eleanor related the conversation she had had with her dad and said she felt he was hiding something. They said their goodbyes in a way that only lovers would, their faces glowing as they parted. Eleanor declined the offer to stay the night at Jonathan's. She was not yet ready, and didn't yet want to tell her dad about the relationship.

It had all been so sudden, too. She felt their relationship needed time and they should slow down, but once with Jonathan she just felt the urge to hold him, kiss him, give herself totally to him. She had desperately wanted to stay at Jon's and regretted her decision to decline the offer. But she felt she needed space and time. Time to reflect. She hoped their relationship had more durability than a passing April shower, but she was desperately afraid that Jonathan would lose interest. She recalled an earlier friendship she had struck with a boy at school. They had had one glorious moment of passion at the back of the school field and then, well, the next day she saw him in the arms of Kelly the most beautiful and popular girl in her class. She remembered her bitter sense of loss and vowed that next time she'd take things more slowly. But this was moving forward at the speed of an out-of-control juggernaut.

Chapter Eleven

It was only in the early evening on Sunday, after her dad had left for London that Eleanor contacted Jonathan on her mobile. They arranged to have a meal together in the Puss in Boots.

That night Eleanor stayed over.

As the first grey light seeped through the thin curtains in Jonathan's bedroom, reluctantly he dragged himself away from the soft sleeping form of Eleanor. He felt he needed a good run and maybe a workout. He kept a gym in the basement which had been rather neglected of late.

Jonathan's routine, mainly in theory rather than practice, was to get up at six for his run on alternate days and although every fibre in his being urged him to stay warm and tucked up in bed with the love of his life, he knew the rewards for his sacrifice would be huge. He would return glowing with his exertion, pleasantly tired and ready for all that the day had to throw at him.

The huge mental effort needed to propel himself out of the door was exacerbated by the leaden skies from which issued a steady drilling rain. He quietly closed the front door behind him and set off at a steady pace towards the village. The relentless rain had returned, making the sunlit Saturday he had spent with Eleanor feel as though it had been weeks ago.

Discovering that the rain didn't unduly affect his performance he increased his pace and soon the village was receding behind him as he ran on to the Beckton road.

On an impulse, as he passed the Council estate, he decided to run around the looped road it was built on. It was generally a neat, well-kept estate and the generous gardens afforded the tenants when the houses were first built had allowed the current occupiers to develop their gardening skills. The front gardens were a riot of colour from spring flowers such as tulips and daffodils. Clematises, climbing roses and honeysuckle smothered the red brick walls. Most of the houses had been bought and the new house owners took pride in keeping them immaculate.

The one exception was the Charles family. Their house was the first in the street abutting the main road and had a larger plot than its neighbours. There was an air of neglect about the house. Long lank grass grew in the front garden and the flower beds, hardly recognizable as such, were choked with weeds. A rusting bicycle lay buried in the grass and, on the front door, the blue paint was peeling. The once white wooden picket fence surrounding the garden was broken and rotting in places.

These details were not what caught Jonathan's eye. There, in the drive to the side of the house, was the white van sporting the red logo *Valentine's Removals*.

So that's who had been driving the van on the day of the captain's demise and also three days ago, when they had left the barn rather hurriedly. Not the terrorists, but Kevin. There was almost certainly a connection. He ran back onto the Beckton Road and onto a bridleway which led through a large field into the Skandlebury Forest.

Trust Kevin to be involved, he thought. He has a finger in most of the criminal enterprises in the area.

Kevin, the handsome blue-eyed local hoodlum. Who did he remind him of? And why the urgent desire to talk with Eleanor? What exactly was Richard Jennings relationship with Kevin and why did he hate him so violently? These questions filled Jonathan's mind as his feet pounded the forest floor.

Ten minutes into the woods, as the sun rose, it dawned on him. He would have to arrange a meeting between Kevin and Eleanor.

Despite the relentless drilling rain, it was quite bright in the woods. Although there were darker fir plantations for commercial logging, the part he was running through consisted mainly of mature oak and birch trees and was pleasantly open and light.

As an intermittent bird watcher, Jonathan was always alert in the countryside to bird and wildlife, so abundant in the area. He was always thrilled to spot deer in the woods or an otter in one of the many brooks in the area. Badger watching in the spring was a delight with the newborn cubs playing outside the setts under the eye of their watchful mother.

He was thus acutely alert to what was going on around him and noticed a slight movement out of the corner of his eye. He saw a black speck a couple of hundred yards away. The urgent metallic chink of the blackbird's warning call rang through the air.

He had company. He looked behind him and caught the flash of what he assumed were binoculars. It was a trap. He cursed himself for not varying his habits more, a basic rule that the army had taught him to avoid danger. It could only be the two who had been hiding in the barn. OAK was closing in on him! They must have known that a run was usually part of his morning routine.

He stopped running, his heart beating fast. His only option was to hide in a place where they would never think of looking and to act fast before they realised that he had become aware of the trap. But where? The pleasant open woodland offered very little scope for hiding. He cast around desperately looking for a suitable oak tree in which to hide.

He made his way to an old tree with wide spreading branches, when details of a history project at school came to mind. The woods had been part of the grounds of the Skandlebury Abbey before the Dissolution in the 1530s. Where the boundary had been was now a shallow ditch filled with leaves and the detritus of centuries. In certain more sheltered places the ditch could still be traced. One such sheltered place was underneath the canopy of an enormous and ancient holly bush a hundred yards to the left of the footpath. Making his way cautiously he slid under the bush, ignoring the painful pricking of the leaves. Lying flat on his belly, he inched further into the densest part. He sank into the shallow ditch. There he could not possibly be seen unless someone took a long hard look under the bush or crawled through the thorns as he had done.

Ten minutes passed. Jonathan remained motionless, ignoring the spider dangling by a thread near his left ear until it landed lightly on his neck and the urge to brush it off became overwhelming. That, and the effort to stifle the sound of his own heavy breathing, was agonizing. Jonathan lay rigid, the spider was now crawling down his bare neck and he was just about to give in to the urge to scratch when a face appeared under the bush. Brown eyes were scanning the forest floor. With every muscle tense, Jonathan lay still.

"Come on, Khalid!" said a voice, "He won't be there."

"I thought I saw a movement."

"Probably a bird or something."

"You're right," said Khalid, and the face disappeared from view.

"What are we going to do? We'll have to tell Nawaf that the rat's escaped. And he won't like that."

"We'll tell Nawaf nothing. After all he doesn't know what we're doing. But he can't be far away."

"He must've managed to get out of the wood somehow."

"Or he's climbed a tree and I don't rate our chances at finding him. Don't fancy a cricked neck either."

"We've got to get him by Saturday," said the other man, whom Jonathan assumed to be Fahad. "Nawaf will tell us what to do. He'll have a better idea than this fiasco. What a waste of time traipsing round this fucking wood. It's all your fault, you know. You wanted to win Nawaf's favour."

"OK, OK," replied Khalid and added, obviously wanting to avoid confrontation, "not one of my better ideas. You're right, I wanted to suck up to Nawaf. He treats me like shit. I figured it's better to catch him early than not catch him at all. After all, Nawaf's in his cricket team. Little does he know what's in store for him. Would love to see his face when he realizes that he'll be blown up with half of Beckton!"

"True, let's hope Plan B works, whatever Nawaf decides. Can't believe he's the same kid that we went on missions with in the desert."

"Well, he always had more brains than us. I'm sure whatever he decides will be better than this crazy plan."

"What about his bitch? Nawaf said we should get her to ensure Chambers' obedience. Yeah we'll see what he's made of when he has to decide between her and half of Beckton."

"She's a bit of alright though, ain't she? I'd like a piece of her."

The two men chuckled.

Their voices receded into the distance, leaving Jonathan in turmoil. He had to protect her from these animals at all costs. This was their typical modus operandi. In Jordan, OAK made a hostage of the police chief and forced him to drive a lorry laden bomb into a hotel where important western diplomats were staying. On that occasion, the bomb had failed to go off, the policeman had jumped out of the vehicle and had been whisked away. The organization was deeply humiliated by this failure.

Now he knew a terrorist act was to take place next Saturday, the police needed to be involved.

Chapter Twelve

There was another blot on Skandlebury's fair landscape, namely Hangman's Lane. The origin of the name is lost in history but it wouldn't take much imagination to formulate a theory. The feeling of gloom that some villagers claimed they got when anywhere near the little lane was attributed to the notorious past assumed in its name. Many local lawbreakers had met their end here and, it was suggested, their tortured souls still haunted the area. This feeling of gloom could also be attributed to the fact that the road had been severely neglected. It was full of giant muddy puddles from the recent rains and grass grew in the cracks of the ancient tarmac. The grass verges now consisted of banks of brambles and thigh high nettles. Very few vehicles went down the lane to serve its two houses. Even the postman left his bike at the beginning of the lane and walked. The first of the houses was a ramshackle decaying cottage with a front garden similarly overtaken by weeds. It was lived in by an old woman called Agnes who only ever left her home to visit the village shop and the church. She was believed to be in her nineties, but no one was sure of her age. She could normally be seen making her way across the green leaning heavily on her walking stick, her back bent, long lank locks of white hair flopping over and partially concealing her ancient, wrinkled face.

The house next door was called The Willows and was a more substantial property. The owner had not returned for years and, according to local gossip, now lived and worked as a head teacher of a private school in Argentina. When the long-term tenant had inexplicably left, Nawaf and his friends hadn't delayed in securing the tenancy for themselves. Invisible from the village road, and with open countryside between the back of the cottage and the railway line, very few people would be aware the house existed, and even fewer that it was occupied by a group of men of Middle Eastern origin.

"So," said Nawaf, surveying the assembled company. "I need progress reports from all of you, and complete honesty."

A group of men were sitting around a large wooden dining table in the bay windowed front room. The air was thick with smoke. They clearly hadn't read the no smoking clause in the lease. There were one or two tense faces. Others feigned relaxation, but there was no doubt who their leader was. Their gaze was fixed, somewhat apprehensively, on the unassuming man with a determined look on his face, sitting at the head of the table, pen poised over a note book.

"Omar," Nawaf said addressing a bearded man with glasses who looked rather like an accountant, "how's the bomb preparation?"

"We have had a few setbacks," replied the man quietly, taking a puff on his cigarette, as if he was talking about a sales campaign in a paper clip company, "but I'm working on it. Give me another week. Our factory was raided by counter-terrorist police in London, but we've found new premises and sourced new material."

Omar paused for a second and then added with a hint of pride. "We've been working round the clock making the new bomb and, if anything, it will be better than the first - lighter, but deadlier."

"OK," Nawaf replied, "It needs to be ready in less than a week - by Saturday – and has to be reliable."

"Yes sir," replied Omar, "there is nothing I don't know about explosives, trust me."

"Good. Nikita," Nawaf now turned to a tall muscular Russian man with a flat nose, "how's plans for the transport coming along?"

"All in order," the man replied in thickly accented tones, "it should be in place within a week as discussed."

Nawaf looked pleased and then fixed Fahad with a steely stare. "How are your plans coming along? You and Khalid were supposed to arrange to kidnap the targets."

Fahad stared at Nawaf like a frightened child who had not done his homework and was facing a stern teacher. "W - we've sorted out some things," he stuttered, "but we need to find a suitable way of kidnapping them. Also, the timing is important: we don't want to have to keep them locked up too long in case they are discovered. Leave it with me."

"You haven't even got a plan, have you? Have you been watching their movements? Have you found a suitable place to hide them? On that point, incidentally I have, and I'll let you know where I want you to keep them in due course. But you've done nothing. At the last meeting I asked you for a plan. Where is it? Why do I let you stay on as part of this group? You and Khalid are useless pieces of shit. The only reason you're still here is that I don't want the bother of killing you both and having to dispose of your miserable corpses."

Nawaf glanced at Nikita, who immediately bunched his fist and smashed it into Fahad's terrified face.

"Idiot," hissed Nawaf, "Too busy playing cards with your stupid friend. I better be able to trust you now though because next time..." he paused, "next time you won't get up."

The blow had been so hard that Fahad, had landed with a thump on the wooden parquet flooring, where he lay whimpering, trying to stem the blood flowing from his nose.

"We can't afford passengers," Nawaf continued. "This is an opportunity to strike a blow at the enemy that will be deadlier than 9/11. Let that be a lesson to all of you. Any slackers, or those who do a bad job..." The sense of menace was palpable.

Khalid who was next to be interrogated, looked on terrified, marvelling at how their relationship had been changed from a gang of mates to being cowed into submission by their cold-hearted erstwhile companion.

"You deserve to be punished too, you fool," he said. "You think this is all a game, don't you?"

It was Khalid's turn to look terrified. Nikita was flexing the muscles of his right arm. "I - I know we haven't made much progress," he stammered, "but we - we've been helping with the raising of finance. Stuck in a barn looking after stuff before it's sold on."

Nikita grunted. "Yes, the delay in getting the transport is down to finance but they tell me the finance will be available soon."

"Yes, yes," said Khalid eager to seize a lifeline, "we've just sold another item for thousands. More than enough to cover the cost."

Nikita looked at Nawaf questioningly, but Nawaf shook his head.

Khalid visibly relaxed.

"Ok, let's go through the plans once again, and close any loopholes..."

Heads were bent over Nawaf's notes as they argued and discussed. The meeting broke up an hour later and Nawaf left the room abruptly without so much as a good night to his fellow conspirators. His contempt for Khalid and Nawaf clearly extended to all his fellow conspirators. He made no effort to conceal it.

Chapter Thirteen

Beckton Police Station was a 1930s building, large, square and of solid red brick construction. It stood imposing on the mainly Tudor and Georgian High Street of the picturesque market town of Beckton, administrative capital of Beckshire.

Jonathan and Eleanor sat in the reception, the walls of which were painted a dull cream. It was a bleak, utilitarian place designed to be purely functional. The only colour came from the numerous posters offering safety advice or requesting information on missing persons or wanted criminals. Behind the low curved wall with a wooden countertop sat the desk sergeant. A stolid, unemotional man who clearly followed procedure with minimal flexibility, he had promised they could see the Inspector as soon as he was available.

In a few minutes they were ushered into the inspector's office.

Inspector Wallis smiled welcomingly across a vast antique oak desk as they entered. There were the inevitable in-trays and out-trays and pending trays on the desk which was scattered with papers just enough to say 'I am a busy man' without saying 'I am untidy and disorganised' or worse still: 'I haven't got enough to do'.

Photographs of his wife and children were also displayed. The walls of his office were decorated with anaglypta cream wallpaper, clearly untouched since at least the 1970s, alleviated only by framed commendation certificates, certificates of courses completed, and another large, framed photograph of his family.

"Sit down. Can I get you a drink?" His attitude was warm and welcoming in contrast to the immovable desk sergeant. The two took their seats on chairs facing the Inspector and politely declined his offer.

"No thanks," said Jonathan, "we have something very important to tell you, and we need your help."

"The point is," added Eleanor in her direct way, "we are terrified that we are being targeted by terrorists. They're planning some outrage involving us. Particularly Jonathan."

The Inspector raised his eyebrows. He clearly was not a man to express his feelings with abandon but Jonathan was puzzled by the lack of surprise in his reaction. "You better tell me what you know," he said.

Between them they told the inspector about Jonathan's family background and the events of the past few days.

The officer listened without interrupting. "So, to sum up," he said, leaning back on his chair, his brown eyes fixed on them, "this Nawaf has been trying to get close to you to involve you in some act of terrorism in Beckton which will result in your death and probably many others too. How can you be so sure?"

"Well, if he just wanted to kill me, he could have done that straight away and, what's more, he wouldn't need a whole team of terrorists to do it. They're living in Hangman's Lane in Skandlebury by the way – The Willows, according to village gossip.

"I overheard them discussing the revenge they would take on me when they tried to trap me in the woods. I've also been following OAK in the news and this sort of revenge is typical. They see it as somehow fitting that their enemies should be forced to be involved in their atrocities."

"Well, thank you for sharing this with us. Excuse me while I make a phone call."

He came back five minutes later with a smile on his face. "It's OK. We'll be sending an extra patrol to the village with special instructions to keep a watch on your house. Try not to go out too much until the danger is passed. Now, if that is all, I'm a busy man and have an extra patrol to organize." Smiling, he led them to the door.

Jonathan and Eleanor left with the distinct feeling that the Inspector was not dealing with their problem with the gravity they felt it deserved. In short, they had been given a polite brush off.

******

The Inspector's officer door had hardly closed behind them when he dialled a number.

"Nawaf?"

"Yes?" said Nawaf on the end of the line.

"As expected, they've come in and told me the whole story."

"Thought they would. What are you going to do?" asked Nawaf.

"We'll set up a patrol to reassure them, but it's down to you take them out."

"Ok."

"I think your suggestion of the castle is good. It's secure and local to you. We'll inform the curator accordingly."

******

Jonathan and Eleanor drove back in silence, hardly reassured by their reception at the police station.

As they approached the village, Jonathan said, "I've invited someone over for tea."

"Oh," said Eleanor, "who?"

"Sorry for not telling you earlier. I'm afraid you might not welcome him, but you must speak to him: he has something important to tell you."

"Who is it?" asked Eleanor again, alarmed.

"Kevin."

Chapter Fourteen

Eleanor found it somewhat incongruous to offer the village tearaway something so civilized as afternoon tea, but Kevin happily munched down a huge slice of the chocolate cake she had bought from the tea shop, accompanied by several cups of sweet, milky tea. The weather had cleared somewhat, and the warm early evening sun slanted onto the rear garden of Two Trees, bathing the patio where they sat in a golden light.

After a few angry words with Jon, she had begrudgingly accepted that the meeting might well help clear a few things up.

Having had his fill of chocolate cake, Kevin, clad in his habitual black leather jacket, leaned back with a sigh.

"So," he said, looking at Eleanor, "you've finally agreed to talk."

"No, no, no," Eleanor replied, "Jonathan, my boyfriend, arranged this meeting. He says you have something important to tell me."

"I think you think that I want to f...- er- date you," said Kevin, altering the word he was going to use, hastily. "Not true - I don't wanna date you, I wanna tell you that you... you're my half-sister!" He slurped another gulp of tea.

There was a stunned silence for a moment.

Eleanor laughed. "You – you're joking! This is ridiculous. I'm nothing like you. Besides, I know who my mother and father are, and they are not yours."

"He's right." Jonathan spoke for the first time, and there was a note of nervousness in his tone, being unsure how Eleanor would react. "His mum is also your mum. You have the same blue eyes the same shaped nose. And seeing you and Kevin together now, it's even clearer to me that you're related. I worked it out when I was out running. If you are brother and sister, it explains some similarities in your appearance, why your dad desperately wanted to keep you apart from him. He was ashamed of himself, and it's why he threatened Kevin."

"But - how come? My mum can't be that awful Mrs. Charles. I'm nothing like her."

"Hey! You're talking about me old ma," interjected Kevin.

"She was beautiful once," said Jonathan, ignoring Kevin, "and your dad was not the only man in the village to be attracted to her. But she seems to have stopped caring for herself now she's older and men are no longer falling at her feet."

Eleanor was pale, her lip quivering. "How come my Dad never told me?"

Kevin spoke again, his rough unpolished voice grating on Eleanor's ears. "Because he's a fucking snob!" he said, this time unrestrained in his language. "After you were born he took custody of you. Me mum already had four kids and didn't want another, so she was happy to let your dad take you. Besides you were a beautiful baby. My mum still has pictures of you. Your dad and his wife, the mother of your little sister, didn't think they could have kids, so she was very happy to adopt such a beautiful baby girl. Then sod's law along comes your sister. Richard wanted to keep it from you. He was ashamed that my mum was yours too, coz she lives on a Council estate. Like I said, he's a snob."

Eleanor began to cry. Jonathan put his arm around her.

"So, Kevin," said Jonathan, "why are you okay about saying this now?"

"Coz I've been blackmailing Richard Jennings," Kevin replied with surprising frankness. "Made quite a bit I have, but he told me at the Easter fete that he couldn't afford to pay me no more and threatened to kill me if I spilled the beans. So, no money no secret. Although I've got other stuff on him," he added darkly.

"I could go to the police, you know. Blackmailing is a criminal offence."

"Go on then," Kevin said, scornfully "I don't care. Air our family's dirty secrets in public, and like I said I've got other stuff on him so he won't be pressing charges. Anyhow I ain't afraid of prison. Got some good mates, as well as a brother in Beckton jail."

"But why has Mrs. Charles not told me?" asked Eleanor in a small voice.

"Obvious, ain't it?" Kevin replied, "She was paid hush money by your family."

Eleanor's face was white, streaked with tears. "This can't be true!" she cried. She got up abruptly, nearly tripping over Sir Lancelot who was under the table, and fled indoors to Jonathan's bedroom, where she flung herself on the bed weeping bitterly. All this was too overwhelming. Her parents lying to her all these years and to find she had a criminal for a half-brother.

"Stay a minute, Kevin," said Jon and rushed upstairs to comfort her.

"My dad's a bastard!" she wept, "I hate him! I'm never going to speak to him again."

Jonathan said nothing for a while but kissed her damp face and put an arm round her heaving shoulders. His heart ached for her. To feel your parents have betrayed you must be almost as bad as losing them.

"I must talk more to Kevin," he said, gently. "You stay here as long as you like."

Kevin was sitting where he had been left. He was smiling. "Didn't take it well, did she? Not surprised. My mum isn't exactly one you can be proud of. And her dad a snobby, lying bastard. Poor girl, eh? Still, I expect you'll look after her. Tell me, what's she like in bed?"

"Cut that out, you empty headed ignorant git." It was all Jonathan could do to restrain himself from striking Kevin across his smirking face. "I never thought you could sink lower than the gutter you are already in, until you tell me you're a blackmailer. I did have some sympathy with you, as a fish out of water in this respectable middle-class area where you stuck out like a sore thumb. But you've lost that. Go crawl back into the gutter from where you came. And watch your back - blackmailers invariably come to a sorry end."

"Cheers," said Kevin grinning, "and thanks for the cake. We must do it again sometime." He picked up another piece and left.

"Actually, wait!" called Jonathan, at his retreating back, "What can you tell me about Valentines Removals and the two men you picked up at the barn?"

This stopped Kevin in his tracks. There was a moment's silence. "Just a business relationship," he smirked. "Nothing to do with you." With that he exited the side garden gate and was gone.

Eleanor appeared at the French doors. Her face was blotchy,

but she had dried her eyes. Jonathan took her hand. "Listen," he said. "Why don't you move in with me permanently? We can make a home here. You needn't live with your dad if you don't want to."

Eleanor was alarmed for a moment. Their juggernaut relationship seemed to be picking up even more speed. "Look," she said, "I don't want to if you are just doing it out of pity."

"Of course not," Jonathan replied, "think of it has a new chapter, a new opportunity."

"Then I'd love to," said Eleanor, smiling, "but I've very little money without my dad paying me an allowance. My mum pays me a bit too but not enough for me to live on. I couldn't afford to live here."

"Nonsense," said Jonathan. "Money is the least of our worries. I have more than enough for both of us."

"But I can't live off charity!" protested Eleanor

"I'm not charity, silly! I'm your boyfriend! And anyway," he added sarcastically, "I'll make you work damned hard! I expect nothing but delicious home cooked meals on my return from wherever I've been!"

"Well in that case I'll move in now!" Eleanor said laughing, noting the twinkle in Jonathan's eye. "Another point, though - would you want Mrs. Charles as your mother-in-law and the rest of her brood as in-laws, too?"

"This has all been a bit sudden," said Jon, "it must be a shock to discover that you're not quite who you thought you were but over time you I'm sure you'll get used to it. Nothing's changed. You're still Eleanor, the girl I've loved since the first time I set eyes on you. The girl that makes me sing love songs in the shower: who has changed my life. I love your blue eyes, your fair hair and your..." He whispered in her ear. Eleanor smiled like the sun breaking through rain clouds, and he added, "I want to spend the rest of my life with you."

Eleanor drew back and looked at him in the eyes. "Is that a proposal?" she asked. "We've only known each other for a few days."

"I suppose it is," he said. "When love strikes you don't need time to sort it out. I am completely certain that you are the one, but you may want to live with me first and if you can bear my bachelor slovenliness then maybe..."

"Well..." she made a pretence of considering. "I'll give it a shot. Your place doesn't look slovenly to me."

"That's only cos Mrs. Drewett comes in twice a week."

"Oh, Betty! I love her. She doesn't suffer fools gladly. I bet she doesn't take any nonsense from you! She used to be my Sunday school teacher when I was little, and a dinner lady at school. I was terrified of her as a kid."

"We'll let her carry on. She needs the money, and it'll mean we won't argue too much over who does the housework."

"I'm sure we'll find plenty else to argue about," grinned

Eleanor.

Jonathan kissed her and said: "But we must be careful. Until the police catch those terrorists we need to stay indoors as much as possible."

"I see," Eleanor's eyes twinkled mischievously, "a lot of time indoors... What on earth shall we do?"

Jon grinned. "I can't possibly imagine. But seriously we must be careful."

"Do you think the police really want to catch them?" asked Eleanor, serious for a moment, although her heart was bursting with barely restrained joy at the thought of moving in with the man she loved. "I was left with the impression that their capture was not a priority."

"Yes, they seemed a bit half-hearted," said Jon, "but maybe they didn't want to alarm us by making it sound like our lives are actually in danger."

"But we are! I mean they had guns! That in itself is a serious offence! They tried to kidnap you or kill you in the woods. They're probably planning a terrorist attack right now that could kill a lot of people. Maybe we should contact the government or someone higher up and get them to believe us!"

"That's a thought," said Jonathan. "Leave it with me. I'll talk to my uncle, my ex- guardian you know, I've been meaning to since we found out that Nawaf is in the village. He's ex- military, ex-secret service. Doesn't talk about it much, but I know he was quite high up. He also told me on my last visit to tell me if anything strange happens. I suppose being stalked by men with guns would come under that heading."

"I think that's a great idea," said Eleanor. "I would feel a little safer if you did. And look!" she exclaimed, sarcastically. "Behold the might of the law!" A lone police car could be seen driving down School Lane slowly and passing the front of the house.

"Well at least they're active," said Jonathan.

Eleanor cleared up the tea things and they stowed the plates and cups in the dishwasher.

"Why don't we collect your tack from the Frobisher place? We didn't get a chance on Friday. It would give us something to do."

"Well," said Eleanor, "I suppose now we have such close police protection maybe we can risk a trip. I must attend to Captain, poor thing. He needs exercising. I also need to collect the rest of my stuff from my dad's place. I want to be out of there before he returns from London. Eleanor changed into some jeans, and they set off together to the Frobisher farm.

"I've never really asked you," Jonathan said, "what are your plans for the future?"

"Oh, I'm planning to go to university. I've taken a year out but want to study English Lit. You know I love poetry and great literature. It is in my blood I suppose. My grandparents also loved it. Must have skipped a generation with my dad, though. I start in September."

Jonathan looked anxious. "Where?"

Eleanor laughed. "Oh, a long way away! The University of Beckton! I'll be home in the evenings. I can even bike it."

Jon breathed an audible sigh of relief. He thought life would not be worth living if he was separated from this beautiful girl who had completely turned his life upside down.

They drove up the long drive to the farm, past the barn where it all began and stopped in front of the farmhouse. The mellow red brick longhouse glowing in the evening sun. They knocked on the oak door.

Chapter Fifteen

The door opened to reveal Mrs. Frobisher. She looked graceful with long slim legs clad in jean shorts and a red T-shirt. She somehow always seemed to look elegant even when she was dressed casually.

"Hi!" she said in a friendly manner. She appeared to have forgotten her earlier suspicions of Eleanor. "Come on in. Can I get you a drink?"

"Oh, no thanks," said Eleanor, "we're just here to collect my tack. I've moved Captain to the paddocks behind Jonathan's house."

"Actually, I wouldn't mind a drink," Jonathan said.

Eleanor glared at Jon, furious at having been contradicted, but nevertheless had no choice but to follow them along an oak paneled corridor. The top of the walls was painted a tasteful olive green, and oil paintings, acquired during the time the Captain had had an art gallery in France, hung along the walls. Mrs. Frobisher led them into a beautiful sitting room.

It was furnished in the English country style with a reproduction Queen Anne sofa and chairs, upholstered in a pink and green floral pattern. An expensive hand knotted silk patterned rug lay over a subdued pink carpet in front of the hearth. More pictures, depicting landscapes and hunting scenes, adorned the walls.

"What do you fancy?" she asked. "I've just opened a bottle of Burgundy."

They duly accepted the offer, and once they were all seated, glasses of wine in hand, she asked: "So, tell me what have you found out about Edwin's death?"

To Eleanor's surprise Jon said: "Well, it definitely wasn't suicide, and I don't think it was an accident. There is no doubt its murder. Your husband was too clever to fall from the hayloft and, as far we know, had no reason to kill himself. Again, if he had wanted to kill himself he wouldn't have jumped from that hayloft but would have chosen a surer method. We found evidence that someone had been using the barn for something and had been sleeping there. I think I know who did it.""

"Really?" said Virginie, her well-manicured eyebrows arching. "Go on."

"Give me a couple of days," Jonathan replied. "I can't say anything until I'm certain."

"That's great news! If you find out I shall be ever so grateful."

"I'll try my best."

They chatted inconsequentially about various things but the talk always returned to Edwin. Virginie seemed genuinely fond of her late husband. Or at least appeared to be trying to make out she was. Eleanor couldn't help remembering the comment Charlie Melville had made, that she didn't seem very upset at his death, or maybe she was just too well bred to show grief in public.

"I suppose it's too early to make plans," said Eleanor attempting to speak gently, "but have you any thoughts as to what you might do in the future? Last time we spoke you were talking of selling the place."

"Yes. I probably will but, as you say, it's still too soon. I might go back to France. My family has a chateau there. Meanwhile I'll stay here and try to get justice for Edwin." There was a definite uncertainty in her tone as she spoke those last words. She lowered her eyes as she spoke, not able to look them in the eye.

Jonathan drained the last drop of his wine and stood up to leave. They said their goodbyes and promised to keep in touch. The sun had almost set as they went into the yard, a globe of blood orange slipping below the horizon.

"Well?" said Eleanor, furiously as they loaded the tack into Jonathan's four by four. "What are you keeping from me? How can you say that we've made progress? We've made no progress since we visited the barn, except to discover that terrorists were hanging out there and were the obvious killers."

"I was acting on impulse when I said what I said to Virginie. I'm not keeping anything from you. I think we've made excellent progress if you look at all the information we have and piece it together. There are a few unanswered questions, such as what were they storing in there, and what, if any, the relationship is between Kevin, your Dad and the terrorists."

"You think Kevin is linked to the terrorists?"

"Quite likely. He's possibly using his van to move stolen or illegal goods that have been temporarily hidden in the barn. And they must be valuable for them to be so closely guarded. I think he's doing that for the terrorists who are obviously making money from some scam or other to fund their plans. I think they're stolen or illegal goods, else why disguise his van? He clearly isn't in the house moving business."

"Yes, that's true," said Eleanor, "I checked the internet and local business directories, and even local newspapers but he doesn't appear to advertise at all."

"That confirms his business is phony. Oh, and I doubt he knows or cares who his bosses are. I'm sure he'll do anything to make money and I bet they pay him well."

"What about my dad?"

"Same thing. He's short of money, after all he is, or was, being blackmailed, and was paying hush money to your real mother. From what I know of him and from what you've told me he too would do anything for money – no questions asked. Perhaps they're paying him for some service or information or something."

"You may be right."

Eleanor remained silent for a moment, contemplating the idea that her Dad was a crook in cahoots with a murderous bunch of terrorists. She was sure though that her father didn't know what they were planning. He may lack scruples but Eleanor felt that if he had known their plans he surely would not have anything to do with them. Money was his only motive and he would not ask questions about what they were up to.

Jonathan paused as he was about to put the last leather saddle in the boot of his car.

"You know," he said, "I've just had a brainwave. Why didn't I think of this before? I need to ask you a big favour. I want to search your dad's house. Do you have the password to his computer?"

"Yes, I do." said Eleanor. "He's not very careful about computer safety. For ages he had his password on a post-it-note stuck to the side of his computer until he memorized it."

"Well, we need to find a physical link between him and Kevin.

Also, I want to check out his business in London. I think Nawaf is quite a sophisticated operator and he'd definitely manipulate the city to his financial advantage using your Dad."

"You could search his office and computer, while I pack my stuff. I don't want to live in the same house as my Dad."

Jonathan smiled. *Can't blame her for being angry*, he thought, *but given time she'll come to terms with her dad – maybe even forgive him*. Though that could be some time, if the thunderous expression on Eleanor's face was anything to go by.

"We'll do that tonight."

The loading completed, Jonathan started the engine and they drove off.

"So, who do you think killed the captain?" asked Eleanor as they drove down the long drive. "Was it the terrorists? Or was it Kevin and my dad that the captain surprised when he was inspecting the barns? After all I did see the van driving away from the farm around the time of Captain Frobisher's death."

"We don't know who was in the van. It could be, and most likely was, Kevin and your dad, but if they were taking a delivery away from the barn, maybe members of the terrorist gang were there too. It's my theory that they've been sleeping there protecting the goods. If they were taken for sale somewhere, there is no need for the gang members to be in the barn. My view is that they were in the van with Kevin, your dad and the stolen goods. I still think it was the terrorists. I can't see your Dad or Kevin, despite their faults, being murderous or supporting a Middle Eastern terrorist campaign against the West."

"But what else is Kevin blackmailing my dad with? What's his *other stuff* he talked about? Maybe he killed Captain Frobisher and Kevin is threatening to tell the police."

"Could be but, as I say, my gut instinct is that neither of them is a murderer. The *other stuff* could be something to do with the trafficking in illegal goods."

"Oh, and by the way," said Eleanor, suddenly. "I got the impression from Virginie that she isn't totally on the level. I think she's hiding something from us."

"Oh, I don't think so," Jonathan replied. "She's probably just a bit unsure about her husband's death – was it murder or accident? Possibly unsure, too, over how much she can trust us to find the truth. Grief can addle the mind."

"No, I think she is hiding something from us," insisted Eleanor, "maybe she knew what was going on in the barn."

"Doubt it, Ellie. She seems genuinely fond of her husband, and anyway, she doesn't seem like the type to be involved with terrorist or racketeers. I think you're a bit jealous of her. Go on," he teased, "admit it."

"Huh!" responded Eleanor scornfully, "what have I got to be jealous of? She is pretty but I think without the makeup and the designer clothes she'd be very ordinary. I think you're smitten with her."

Jonathan laughed. "Of course not." To Eleanor his denial sounded hollow.

"Look," said Eleanor, "you're only a bloke. It's a man thing to like a pretty woman. It's in your DNA. I would be surprised if you didn't fancy her a bit."

"OK," admitted Jon with a sigh, "I admit she's good looking, but I find her a bit cold, if you know what I mean. I suppose I admire her like I would a fine painting or a glorious cover drive."

Eleanor didn't reply and they drove in silence. After a while Jonathan found the silence awkward. "Are you all right?" he asked.

"Yes," she sighed, "Just wondering what a cover drive is."

Once back at Two Trees, they unloaded the tack into the shed in the paddock. It was tiring work as they had to carry the tack from the front drive across the garden through a gate and across the paddock to a shed in the far corner. Captain looked on munching hay, indifferent as his mistress struggled with a heavy saddle across the field. He seemed quite at home in the new paddock.

Feeling tired after a long day they decided to spend the evening in and postpone their visit to Bulmer Cottage. After feeding Sir Lancelot, they ordered pizzas from Beckton which they ate together in the cosy lounge. Jonathan got bored with a rather long, romantic film on TV with which Eleanor was absorbed. Something was bothering him about the whole affair. That barn had seemed very busy on the morning of Edwin's death.

He went upstairs to his study where he kept a copy of the police file. He read through the notes carefully and then found what he was looking for. They had been so unbelievably stupid. The answer had been staring him in the face! He leapt up and dashed downstairs and called out: "I need to ask Virginie a few questions. See you later!" and before she could answer he had grabbed his car keys and was on his way out.

Eleanor was puzzled. She switched off the television - the film had ended - and sat back in her chair. Why the rush? What had he found out that she didn't know? Wasn't it a bit late in the evening to visit an attractive widow uninvited? She suddenly felt scared. She shook her head, as if to try and rid herself of the feeling. "This is silly," she said aloud, "she is a lovely lady who's just lost her husband." Anyway, what had she to gain from her husband's death? Well, other than an estate worth a million or maybe more. Suppose she had killed the Captain for his money? She could be dangerous. What had Jon said when they first met? *A person who has killed once won't hesitate to do so again if they feel threatened.*

Eleanor felt panic rising inside her and for a moment was frozen in an agony of indecision. On the one hand she didn't want to appear to be making a fuss over nothing, but on the other hand maybe Jonathan had found something and was off to confront her. Maybe even accuse her of murder. If she had killed once, she wouldn't hesitate to kill again. Then with an overwhelming sense that Jonathan was in danger, she made up her mind. Five minutes later she was speeding down School Lane, her slim legs pumping up and down manically as she drove her bike faster and faster.

She took the corner at the bottom of School Lane far too fast and her bike skidded on a patch of gravel. For several agonizing moments she clung to her bike fighting to keep it upright, but the forces of gravity prevailed, and she was flung onto the road. Her body slid along the road surface, and she hit her head on a white bollard on the edge of the common.

Everything went black.

Chapter Sixteen

For the second time that day, Jonathan's Range Rover's tyres crunched over the gravel drive of the Frobisher farm. His mind was in turmoil. If, as he suspected, she had killed her husband, was he walking into danger? Should he take a weapon with him? No, he was being ridiculous. She was a defenceless woman. To kill her husband, she had to push him out of a hayloft. She didn't use a gun or a knife and what she had done she probably now bitterly regretted.

Partially comforted by this conclusion, though fearing she might have an accomplice, Jonathan selected a claw hammer from his tool box. He concealed it somewhat awkwardly in an inner pocket of his waxed jacket. He removed his mobile phone in the process and, on an impulse, paused to check it for messages before putting it in his trouser pocket. He made his way to the front door. Virginie opened to his tentative knock almost immediately, as if she was expecting him. Jon's mouth fell open. She was obviously dressed for bed and hadn't bothered to put on a dressing gown. She was wearing an ensemble consisting of a cream silk top, partially unbuttoned, and showing more of her cleavage than Jon would want to see without feeling uncomfortable. A pair of matching silk cami-knickers exposed her smooth slim legs.

"I thought it would be you," she said. From behind her back she produced a small pistol. She pointed it directly at him. "You've worked out who killed my husband and that's why you're here. For your information the gravel outside provides ample warning of anyone approaching." With a wave of the pistol, she indicated he should go to the lounge where they had been earlier that day. He had no choice but to obey.

"Sit down," she commanded, the pistol still pointing at Jonathan's chest.

He sat on the sofa, and she arranged herself opposite him in an armchair. He hoped she wouldn't insist on the removal of his jacket within which lay his only means of self-defence.

"So," Jonathan demanded, "why did you kill your husband?"

She did not answer for a moment, then said: "Aren't you

supposed to be begging for your life? I can't let you leave here alive, you must know that."

Jonathan paled as he realised he had walked into a situation that, for him, could only end in death, at least if Virginie got her way.

"Yes, I suppose I do," Jonathan replied, determined not to show fear, "but before you do, please tell me why you killed your husband."

The woman laughed.

"For money," she said, "pure and simple. For the couple of million pounds his estate is worth."

"But I thought you loved Edwin."

"Yes, I suppose I did... but I love the money far more! You do realise this is clearly not my first murder. I killed my previous husband in France. Mind you that was easy. He was a fat, lazy womaniser. Very rich, of course, or so I thought. I felt nothing for him. In fact, I hated him. I think I married him solely for the money. He fell off his horse after I cut the saddle strap. Again, it looked like an accident. While he was lying on the ground, I bashed his head in with a rock and then arranged the body to look like he had fallen off and hit his head. I also replaced the saddle I'd sabotaged with another one – very clever I thought. To the police it was an accident and they never bothered to investigate properly. If they had done, they would have found the damaged saddle buried in the woods nearby."

She looked at Jonathan as if she expected him to admire her cleverness. Jonathan kept his face expressionless, only its pallor betraying his fear. She took a sip of wine from a half empty glass on the coffee table and then continued, the gun never wavering.

"I inherited his estate, but unfortunately I hadn't realised that he was up to his eyeballs in debt, and I got virtually nothing. I was bitterly disappointed but at least I got out of an awful marriage. He really was a dreadful man. I was determined to do better next time."

"So how did you meet Edwin?"

She sighed. "So-o-o romantic! Soon after my first husband's death I was drinking coffee in a Parisian café and Edwin came in. He looked gorgeous. Immaculate in his grey silk business suit and royal blue tie. He saw me and sat down at my table. It was love at first sight! For him I mean. I don't fall in love *that* easily. I liked him, of course, but he was besotted with me. We had a romantic dinner in Le Train Bleu at the Gare de Lyon. After a few weeks he asked me to marry him. I'd ascertained he was very wealthy and owned an art gallery in the South of France and that he had inherited a large sum of money from his father, who had died recently. I said yes, partly because he was clearly totally in love with me, and because he was rich. I thought I could do much worse. I find English gentlemen so sexy. He had been in the army and was tall, upright, and handsome. We got married and Edwin, who was a little homesick, decided that he wanted to return to

England. He sold his art gallery and we bought Pollards Farm."

"And then you decided to do away with him and get the money?"

"Not so fast! For a while we were happily married and yes, I think I had begun to fall in love with him. He was such a gentleman! So kind and considerate. He let me choose the interior designs for this house and oversee its renovation while he played the gentleman farmer."

"So, for a while we lived together happily enough. And then he had this crazy idea of converting the barns into holiday homes. He would have had to borrow money on our property and the conversion costs would have been enormous. It would have been years before we got a return on our investment, if ever. I mean who would want to come to this God forsaken place for a holiday?"

"So you decided to kill him?" Jonathan was watching Virginie for a moment of inattention, but she continued to point the gun, unwavering, at his chest.

"Well, it crossed my mind at the time. But I was weak. As I say, I'd begun to fall in love with him."

"What happened next?"

"Well, he persisted with the idea, and was so enthusiastic. He appointed an architect who surveyed the barns. The architect drew up plans and Edwin persuaded me to come on a tour. He wanted me to share his vision, you see. The barn where he died was the last we visited. By this time, far from sharing his vision, I was convinced it was going to cost a fortune. He talked of high-end kitchens, and bathrooms, and ecofriendly heating systems. So, as we climbed into the hayloft in that last barn, I was really angry and confronted him. I said it was all an expensive mistake and no way could I agree to the scheme. He went all cold and angry and made for the loft opening without saying a word. He always had been a man of few words. I couldn't resist pushing him. He fell through the gap and that was it. A bonus was that he bashed his head and that killed him. Saved me finishing him off, like I had to with my first husband." She gave a cruel laugh, and harsh lines marred the beauty of her face.

"So that, darling boy, is the truth. You can call me a black widow if you like. I prefer praying mantis. You're a handsome young man. When I first saw you in the barn, I wanted you. There's no denying you will be my next victim. You will make love to me and then I'll kill you quickly. The praying mantis always kills her mate after making love. If you refuse to make love I'll begin with your kneecaps. There are six bullets in this gun - only the last will kill you." She stood up and deftly undid another button with her free hand, revealing more cleavage, still pointing the gun at Jonathan's chest. Despite his horror of the situation there was no denying her attractiveness. It still wasn't enough to stop panic rising in his throat.

"Interesting," said Jonathan, swallowing hard to keep the

panic down. "How can you 'make love' and point the gun at me at the same time?"

"Mmm... let me think." Virginie pretended to think. "I'm sure we'll find a way."

"You're mad," said Jonathan. "Do what you will but I'm loyal to Eleanor."

"Oh, that silly little girl you drag around with you?" Virginie sneered. "Edwin was fond of her too. I'm sure he had his way with her."

"He loved her like a daughter," said Jonathan, "only your sick mind would imagine anything else."

"Enough!" she was leaning forward now, angry and threatening. Jonathan looked away. The sight of her cleavage, far from arousing him, actually sickened him.

"Get up," she commanded, "and undress! Oh, and I know what you're thinking," she added with a sneer, "but make one false move and I'll shoot."

Feeling like he was in a bad erotic novel, or a cheap 1970s soft porn film, Jonathan slowly obeyed, removing his jacket, which he slung over the arm of the chair, the claw hammer in the inside pocket now visible and very accessible.

He was about to remove his trousers when there was a loud banging at the door. Virginie turned in the direction of the noise giving Jon the opportunity he needed. In one swift movement he took the claw hammer from his jacket pocket and smashed it into her head. She sank unconscious to the floor, dark blood spurting from the wound, pooling on the priceless Persian carpet.

Jonathan seized her gun and rushed to open the front door.

Chapter Seventeen

The executive committee of Skandlebury Cricket Club was relaxing in the Puss-in-Boots after their monthly meeting. Much of the decision making had been a formality: to appoint officers of the Committee, confirm the minutes of the last meeting and approve amendments to the fixture list, as well as prepare for the Annual General Meeting, traditionally held at the end of May. Nawaf was welcomed to his first meeting and a presentation was made to Arthur Caldwell, the retiring captain.

Mike Jones was limiting himself to one whisky as he had driven to the pub straight from work and didn't want to be caught drink driving. Along with Nawaf, Arthur Caldwell and

Claire Stokes, the vicar's daughter, who acted as Treasurer and Secretary, were present. She was drinking white wine and telling a funny story about a customer in the teashop. Nawaf was staring inscrutably into space, seemingly detached from what was going on around him. A couple of the other members of the committee had gone outside for a smoke.

Mike Jones' phone rang. He eventually located his phone in one of his pockets and answered, "Hi love."

There was a pause as he listened to what his wife had to say.

He turned to the assembled company "Sorry chaps and chapess. Must dash. One of the kids is ill and I have to collect a prescription from the 24-hour chemist in Beckton."

He left the pub and went to his car, parked under the cherry trees, their blossom ghostly in the gloaming of that balmy spring evening. Something caught his eye across the green near to the school; something moving in the road. He thought it might be a cat, but, straining his eyes, he realized it was too big for that. It appeared to be human. With some trepidation, wondering what he would witness, he got in his car and drove the few yards to the school and stopped. A bicycle was blocking the road, its front wheel still spinning, and not far away was Eleanor, trying to get up from her prone position. He rushed over to her.

"Eleanor, dear!" he cried, "Are you all right?"

Eleanor was in too much pain to answer with anything more than a groan.

Mike squatted down beside her and cradled her head in his lap. There was a cut on her forehead which was oozing blood. He pulled a tissue from his pocket and cleaned the wound. It didn't seem too deep but there was a lot of blood. Mike wasn't sure what to do next, having had few opportunities in his life to rescue distressed maidens and only a sketchy idea about first aid. He gingerly felt each of her legs and arms to check if they were broken, but she seemed to be intact. There was severe grazing down her left arm, which looked worse than it was. Her left thigh was bleeding too, but her jeans had saved her from the worst of it.

He moved the bike from the middle of the road and gently picked Eleanor up in his arms and carried her over to his car.

"Please, please!" she cried, "We have to go to Pollards farm. Jon's in danger!"

"But you need the hospital, you're hurt."

"No! To the farm or Jon'll be killed!" He saw the distress and fear in her face as he laid her down on the back seat of his car and made up his mind. He dialed 999 and asked for the police to go to Pollards Farm where there was a murderer on the loose. He didn't want to add to Eleanor's distress by probing for details. He wondered whether her dazed mind was playing tricks on her. He couldn't imagine for one moment there was any danger at Pollards Farm. You couldn't get a more peaceful, pastoral spot. Nevertheless, he drove in that direction, reassured that the police would respond very promptly, but at the same time feeling slightly guilty of exaggerating the situation to evoke a rapid response.

As Mike approached the farm, he saw police car lights flashing in his rearview mirror. Mike pulled over as much as he could in the narrow lane to allow the police car to pass. Once it had, Mike resumed, tailing the squad car.

"Please tell me what's happening," said Mike to the recumbent Eleanor as they drove down the long drive, "I need to brief the police."

Eleanor struggled into a sitting position, her head thumping madly. "We think Virginie murdered her husband. Jon went to confront her, and I'm afraid she might kill him!"

This is crazy, thought Mike, as an image of the elegant French lady floated into his head: she wouldn't hurt a fly. The police car had drawn up well short of the farmhouse and Mike parked his car behind them. As if by mutual agreement they got out of their cars and Mike told the constable what Eleanor had said.

His reaction was much like Mike's. "This is preposterous," the officer said, "I'm sure Mrs. Frobisher's harmless, but I guess we should check it out."

The moon, almost full, had just come out from behind a cloud and the farmhouse was bathed in milky light. It was very quiet: so quiet they could hear an owl hooting in the woods two fields away. The whole scene was a picture of moonlit tranquility.

Leaving Eleanor in the car, they walked quickly but quietly across the graveled drive and knocked on the door. Both were a little shamefaced at the thought of unnecessarily bothering a single lady, recently bereaved, so late in the evening.

There was a pause. Then a thud. Seconds later the door was flung open by a pale and shaken Jonathan, a gun in one hand.

"Mike! PC Cunningham! Thank God! I think I've killed her!"

"Virginie threatened me with that gun and I hit her with a hammer," he added. "We need an ambulance. She's in the lounge." He showed the astonished policeman the way. Mike was not sure what to do but followed them in anyway.

Virginie lay where she had fallen, blood from her head wound thickening on the rug.

PC Cunningham knelt beside her and felt for a pulse. "She's still alive," he said. "Call for an ambulance." Mike duly obliged. PC Cunningham radioed HQ to inform them that armed officers were not needed.

"Now, Jonathan," he said, "you're in shock. But please explain as best you can why I shouldn't arrest you for attempted murder..."

"Hang on," interjected Mike, "that's crazy. If he had wanted to kill her, he could've used the gun, and anyway Jon wouldn't hurt a fly – unless he had a cricket ball in hand."

"...and illegal possession of a firearm," the policeman continued, not amused by Mike's clumsy and inappropriate attempt at humour.

Jonathan collapsed onto the sofa struggling to gain his composure; he had to work out what to tell the policeman and what to leave out. He didn't want to get sidetracked by having to explain the link with terrorism and in any case, he assumed Cunningham had been briefed on the reason for the extra patrols. The terrorist threat remained the elephant in the room.

There was silence. As Jonathan struggled to compose himself, Mike and the policeman looked on, both hardly able to believe what had happened.

Jonathan began by saying that he and Eleanor had been suspicious about the death of Edwin Frobisher and decided to investigate. He explained how they had found evidence that someone else had been in the barn, possibly staying overnight, and had thought that maybe he had been murdered upon stumbling on their illicit activities.

"We were so sure this was the answer that we almost closed off our investigation. Any way, tonight I suddenly had doubts about the timing of the murder/accident. We'd been to see Virginie and Eleanor thought she was hiding something from us. So, once back at home I looked at the police file again."

"How...?" began PC Cunningham.

"Don't ask!" Jonathan replied. "Eleanor was the key witness in all of this. She had seen a van drive off and we assumed, for reasons I won't go into now, that the van contained the men who had been using the Frobisher barn for illegal activities. This was about 10 am, well before the estimated time of death at 11am, so they couldn't have been involved in his death. Now I know estimates of time of death are inaccurate, but the forensic report indicated the body was still warm when it was found. No one else had been seen by Eleanor or, for that matter, Charlie that morning and indeed there was no reason for there to be anyone *except* Virginie on the farm on the morning of the Easter fete. It was Saturday and the only farm worker, Charlie Melville, had the day off and in fact was at the fete in Bellhinton. Virginie had apparently discovered the body and reported his death at around midday. She had been the only person on the farm, apart from the deceased, the whole morning unless there was a mysterious accomplice. So, on an impulse, and feeling like I had enough evidence, I confronted Virginie, and she threatened me with a gun. When she got distracted by you knocking on the door, I hit her with the claw hammer I had taken with me in case of danger. So thank you. You saved my life."

"All very good," said PC Cunningham, "and all very plausible, but where's the evidence? When she comes round, she'll deny everything, claim the gun was for self-defence and that you threatened her. She'll point to the coroner's inquest that concluded that her husband's death was a tragic accident; nothing to do with her. If the gun is found to be hers, the only charge she'll face is one of illegal possession of a firearm."

The corners of Jonathan's mouth twitched in a small smile of triumph.

"Well, you see," he said, "I recorded our conversation on my mobile phone, during which she not only confessed to the murder of Edwin but also to that of her previous husband in France."

There were gasps of astonishment from Mike and the policeman.

"Good lad," the latter exclaimed, as Jon handed over his phone. "We'll play it now before the ambulance arrives. It will help me decide if your story stacks up and whether I need to arrest you. Here, how do you work this thing?" Jonathan took it from him and set off the recording. Mike and the officer listened, fascinated, to the conversation. When it came to her plans for the killing of Jonathan after enforced sex, Mike allowed himself a smile despite the tragedy of the situation. *What a way to go!* he thought. Later in the pub his account of this had his drinking mates in riotous laughter and many a smutty joke was made at Jonathan's expense.

Just at that moment they heard footsteps in the passage from the front door and Eleanor appeared, white faced, a massive bruise on her forehead, her blouse and jeans torn.

"Ellie!" cried Jonathan, as he rushed to her flinging his arms around her. She grimaced with pain, as he brushed against her grazes.

"Sorry Jon," said Mike, "I should have explained that it was your loyal and caring lady who organised the rescue party."

"But how...?"

"I fell off my bike," Eleanor answered, "and Mike rescued me – and you by the looks of it. Is she dead?"

Just at that moment her question was answered by a groan from the floor.

"Look," said Mike, "why don't I take Ellie to the hospital for a checkup? She won't want to ride in the ambulance with Virginie, I'm sure. My poor wife must be wondering where I am. I promised to get her medicine for my boy. The 24-hour pharmacy is quite near the hospital, so it won't be a bother."

"Good idea," said Jonathan, "I'm probably needed down at the police station anyway."

******

It was gone midnight, before the party had finally broken up. Mike drove Ellie to the hospital. PC Cunningham radioed a colleague to assist him, and the colleague accompanied Virginie to the hospital. The officer drove Jon to the police station, insisting that he would be too shaken up to drive himself. Jon gave a statement and PC Cunningham then drove him back to Pollards Farm so he could collect his vehicle and drive home, the several cups of sweet tea he had been given helping to calm his nerves. Mike did his errand of mercy for his son while Eleanor was being treated at the hospital for her grazes and warned that she might have headaches from possible minor concussion, but nothing to worry about. Mike then drove her back to Two Trees, where he helped her into bed.

As for Virginie, she recovered from her head wound during her stay in hospital under police guard. For her the gloomy prospect of a trial awaited and the inevitable sentence of many years in prison.

******

Some miles away, on the other side of the village, Kevin had made what may well have been his very last delivery.

Chapter Eighteen

Eleanor and Jon were both exhausted and still in shock over the dramatic events of the previous day. Their sleep was troubled and several times Eleanor felt in danger from Jonathan's flailing arms as he tossed and turned.

Eleanor awoke first to yet more rain pounding on the window. It was nearly midday. She sat up in bed, relieved that her head felt better, but she swallowed a couple more paracetamol anyway.

She thought she would get dressed and go downstairs to make coffee but realised she had no clean clothes left. They would have to fetch the rest of her belongings from her father's house. She was wearing a pair of baggy pyjama shorts and donned the least smelly of her tops, her nose wrinkling in disgust.

Jonathan awoke at that moment, glad to be alive. His sleep had been disturbed by images of Virginie pointing an unrealistically large gun at him. In his nightmares she seamlessly changed into Nawaf who chased him through the desert, threatening to kill him with a cricket bat.

"Hey, how are you?" Eleanor said

"I'm fine," Jon replied, sitting up in bed, "how's your head?"

"It's OK. Still throbbing a bit," said Eleanor, before adding: "By the way we must get my stuff today. I've had to wear the same clothes again."

Jonathan cast a critical eye over Eleanor. She had a bandaged forehead. Her damaged arm and thigh had been cleaned, all the gravel removed, and the grazes were already scabbing over.

"You'll live," he smiled at her." Let's go and get your stuff. I don't think I can stand the smell!"

Eleanor cuffed him playfully and they went down to the kitchen for a coffee. It was Eleanor's turn to look at him appraisingly. He was only wearing boxer shorts and his muscled arms and torso were evidence of a man in the peak of fitness.

"I can see why Virginie wanted you," she said, as she put water in the coffee machine, "you, my darling, are gorgeous."

"Thanks," replied Jonathan, trying to sound modest, "I have this problem with women - they just throw themselves at me."

Eleanor laughed. "Or throw themselves off bicycles in an

attempt to save you from a French femme-fatale!" Jonathan laughed and busied himself making coffee. They sat drinking it on kitchen stools.

"You know, despite all that's happened," proclaimed Jonathan, "I feel good. I feel good because we've solved this case and we've brought to justice someone who otherwise would have got clean away with the crime. We made a few wrong assumptions, but we got there in the end and although the case wasn't that difficult, we achieved something the police didn't."

Eleanor smiled, pleased he was in an upbeat mood. "We make a great team. Maybe another case will come our way."

"That would be good. You know, I feel like one of those knights of old who did good deeds and rescued maidens in distress."

"Or, in your case, bop them over the head with a claw hammer!"

They both laughed at this, and it was a relatively cheerful couple, who a few minutes later headed for the door, Eleanor feeling somewhat inappropriately dressed for the weather. Jon lent her a coat and he put on his waxed jacket.

"This case is far from over, though," Jonathan remarked. "We still need to find out what your dad and Kevin are up to and avoid the terrorists, at least until Saturday when their plan is supposed to happen. We've told the police all we know and surely they're working behind the scenes to protect us."

In their upbeat mood they felt that with police protection any attempt at a terrorist outrage would be thwarted, and they had nothing further to worry about. They anticipated the terrorists would any day be arrested and Nawaf and his gang put out of harm's way for a very long time. They had informed the police of all they knew, and it was inconceivable they were not now monitoring the house in Hangman's Lane.

"I'll talk to my uncle when we get back, to see what he makes of it all."

"Thank you darling," said Eleanor. "You know, I have a feeling that our ordeal is almost over and we can really start living again."

She had no idea how completely wrong she was.

Jonathan parked the car by the green. Eleanor opened the door and they entered the quaint little cottage. Bulmer cottage was an end of terrace 18th century farm worker's cottage. They would have been the cheapest and meanest house in the village then, but now they had been smartened up, with some being bought by city dwellers as weekend retreats.

Eleanor immediately went upstairs where she had a shower and changed into clean clothes. She began packing her belongings into two suitcases and she arranged her precious books, many of them required reading for her forthcoming literature course, into several cardboard boxes that she found in the shed in the small back garden.

Jonathan armed with Richard Jennings's password, which

Eleanor had readily given him, went into his office and set to work. The office was furnished simply. There were two shelves on the wall with files. A large desk dominated the room and on it was a computer. Next to the desk was a table containing an all-in-one printer, copier and scanner. There were no photos of loved ones or any ornaments; it was a purely functional workspace. Richard clearly prioritised his business over everything else.

First, he searched the drawers of the desk to no avail. They contained stationery and, rather oddly, a few photos of Greek and Roman antiquities. He pulled some files down from a shelf. Opening the first one, he was puzzled for a moment. The file appeared to be full of certificates of some sort. Examining them more closely he noted they had been signed and stamped by the Turkish authorities. Light dawned. They were certificates of authenticity issued by the Turkish government which allowed the transport of antiquities. The certificates were only issued once the authorities had been satisfied that they had not been stolen.

So far, so legitimate. He then turned on the desktop computer, entered the password and immediately Richard's email appeared. He had not properly shut down the computer from its last use.

Jonathan scrolled through the email feeling twinges of guilt as he did so. The man was clearly having an affair with a woman named Josie with whom he corresponded in long and intimate emails. He was sickened at the hypocrisy of the man who was also writing to his wife whom he variously called 'darling', and 'my love'.

He stiffened as he saw an email had been written to someone named Abdullah: in fact, there was whole file of correspondence. As he read them, what they were up to became depressingly apparent. Richard was informing Abdullah of the arrival of a consignment of antiquities that would be picked up by a man named Ismail. Ismail would meet Kevin at a service station on the M25. These were then transferred to the barn. Richard's job was to connect the antiquities with buyers in London. His company, Jennings Investments, received a fat commission and the rest of the proceeds from sales were passed on to an account which Jon assumed was for the terrorists' use. He then read an email addressed to 'Red Fox'. *Have you printed the certificates for the Zeus statue yet? It is now urgent. I have a buyer for it who won't wait.* The certificates were forged!

Jonathan sat for a few moments at the desk, thinking. Richard was certainly not the sort of father one would wish for. He could shield Eleanor from the affair but his criminal activities would have to be exposed. It was also very clear that Kevin had plenty of material with which to blackmail Richard, particularly if he knew of his extramarital activities. Kevin himself was probably completely in the dark as to what was in the containers that he handed over to Ismail, no doubt in exchange for a generous fee to keep his mouth shut.

Jonathan decided to copy the most damning evidence and submit it to the police: let them deal with it. They had faced enough danger and to meddle in the business affairs of criminals and terrorists would be asking for trouble.

"Eleanor," he called up the stairs, "have you got a flash drive?"

"Yes, be with you in a sec!"

She clattered down the stairs with her two suitcases and handed Jon a flash drive. He quickly copied the most important and damning emails and photocopied a few of the certificates. He left the computer as he had found it.

"I think we have all we need," he said, "Let's go. I'll explain to you in the car."

Eleanor left a note on the kitchen table, curt and without explanation: 'Dad I am moving in with Jonathan." She did not sign her name. In place of a signature, she wrote 'Kevin's half-sister'. Eleanor's belongings were soon stowed in the car and they drove off. Jon explained to his horror-stricken girlfriend what he had found, sparing the details of her father's affair.

"What amazes me," Jon concluded, "is how brazen he is. I suppose hiding away in this sleepy village where policing is negligible, he felt safe and confident enough not to bother hiding the evidence."

Eleanor felt miserable again, her earlier upbeat mood evaporating. How she hated her dad!

"What are we going to do?" she asked, "shall we go to the

police?"

"I think so, but first let's go home have a bite to eat. You can unpack your stuff. I just need to grab some supplies at the shop".

Chapter Nineteen

The reception at the police station late that afternoon was very much different from their previous visit. Detective Inspector Wallis was full of praise for their efforts in bringing Virginie to justice and he reassured them that they were making progress on investigating probable future acts of terrorism. Tight security would be even tighter when the King visited Lower Beckton Wharf to open the new shopping centre on Saturday.

This took both Jonathan and Ellie by surprise. "The King's visiting Beckton on Saturday?" gasped Jon, "surely he must be their target!"

Eleanor turned white. "You must stop them!" she said. "It all fits in now! Revenge on Jon, and a Royal visit to inflict terror on! A neat package!"

"Don't worry!" the Inspector reassured them, "we have everything under control!"

Like the Frobisher case, thought Jon, biting his lip to stop the words coming out.

"Yeah, like the Frobisher case," said Eleanor.

The Inspector smiled ruefully. "We didn't cover ourselves in glory there but, believe me everything is being done to ensure the visit goes smoothly. It's largely out of our hands of course. The King is too important a person to be left to us country bumpkins. Anyway, what can I do for you?"

"Well," began Jon, "when we were investigating the case it was clear someone else was using the barn and, as I think you know, we suspected it was the very terrorists we've told you about. We now know they were using the barn to store Middle Eastern artefacts with false certificates of approval which they would then sell using a city broker who would be paid a fat commission."

"Where's your evidence for that?"

"Here," said Eleanor and handed him the flash drive and a folder. "My father Richard Jennings is the middleman. We raided his office and copied all the relevant documents, plus photos of the stolen artifacts."

The inspector whistled. "Congratulations! So your father's involved? What about family loyalty, eh?"

"That stopped," replied Eleanor scornfully, "when I found out he was just a money grabbing crook. Oh, and my half-brother Kevin is also involved, though mainly in transporting the stolen goods from their point of access into the country to a temporary storage facility – i.e. the Frobisher farm and then onto customers with the necessary forged certificates of authenticity."

The inspector smiled. "This is the last link in the chain. We know who the terrorists are. We think we know what they are planning, and now we have the source of funding. Well done you two!"

"You'll want to speak with *Jennings*," said Eleanor, stressing the surname contemptuously. "On his emails he writes to his floozy Josie. He's going to meet her in Beckton tomorrow night. I'm sure he'll be back in the cottage in Skandlebury, sometime tomorrow."

"You know he was having an affair?" Jonathan looked aghast. "I've been trying to keep it a secret from you."

"Oh, I had a quick look through his emails while you were loading the car with my stuff. It doesn't surprise me: he's always flirting with other women. I'll tell Mum – it will soften the blow when he's jailed to know what a complete and utter slimeball he is!"

"Thank you for that," said D I. Wallis, "we can pick him up any time with the cooperation of the London police. I think you two have done very well and I want to thank you once again.

I'm sure we'll soon round up the terrorists and block their little money-making scam."

He rose from his chair as if to dismiss them. The two left, pleased at what they had achieved and satisfied at DI Wallis's reassurance that they would soon be rounding up the terrorists.

"How did we miss the fact that the King was visiting Beckton?" asked Eleanor as they walked down Beckton High Street to the carpark.

"Well, I've never been one to follow local news very closely and there was no mention of it in the nationals," Jonathan said, "but I do seem to remember talk of it in the pub some while back. I just never thought to make the link."

"And I've been too busy with stuff in Skandlebury, like my horse and the Easter fete, not to mention the Frobisher murder, to pay close attention to Beckton news. Nothing of any real interest normally happens around here."

"We're idiots, though," laughed Jon, "look at all the bunting that's around us. It must have been there yesterday when we were in Beckton, and we never wondered why."

"Yeah, and Beckton looks unnaturally spotless! No litter, and the floral display says: 'Welcome Your Majesty', with the royal coat of arms," Eleanor said, pointing at the patch of green in front of the Town Hall, "bit of a giveaway that!"

"Oh, well," said Jon, "at least we know what the target is, but how on earth will they be able to get past the tight security?

They're bound to close off the roads and put up a very tight cordon around the place. Not to mention intelligence officers in the crowd. They'll never get away with it."

******

In that incident packed week, moments of peace were rare, but they spent the evening at home, relaxing in front of a roaring fire and celebrating the fact that their problems were over. Soon they would look back and revel in their adventures.

It had turned quite cold, true to the fickle nature of an English spring, and frost lay on the ground the next morning as they walked down to the village to buy some milk and bread.

What a sight met their eyes!

Police cars with flashing lights had converged on the village green, an ambulance had drawn up, its rear doors already open wide to receive the injured; a young man, lying still and deathly pale on a stretcher.

Jonathan went over to a policeman and asked what happened. "Young man attacked on the green," he replied, "maybe you can help us. Name's Kevin. We've arrested a man. Before slipping into unconsciousness the lad named his attacker as a Mr. Jennings."

"That's my dad," said Eleanor, shocked, "and Kevin is my half-brother. Will he be ok?"

"Not sure, miss," said the policeman. "If you are next of kin maybe you'd like to ride in the ambulance with him."

"Can I?" asked Eleanor, and her voice was full of concern. Jonathan ran up to the ambulance and obtained the necessary permission and Eleanor climbed into the back where Kevin's stretcher had been placed.

As the doors closed Jonathan smiled to himself, despite the gravity of the situation. Despite all he's done she still loves him, he thought as the cliché of blood being thicker than water sprang to mind. His last glimpse of her was of her grasping the hand of her half-brother as the doors slammed shut and the ambulance sped off.

Jonathan rushed home, got in his car and drove to the hospital.

As he entered the ward, he saw Eleanor sitting at Kevin's bedside still holding his hand and chatting to him. Kevin lay still with his eyes shut, the gash on his forehead, caked with drying blood, contrasted his chalk white face.

Eleanor looked up as he came and sat down in the vacant chair next to her.

"What have they said?"

Well, the doctor examined him and said he'll pull through, but they're not sure whether there'll be any serious damage. Apparently, my dad hit him with a spade, shouting he was ruined."

"Blackmailing is a dangerous occupation," Jonathan said, "but I think your dad deserves what's coming to him. I can't believe he didn't know he was helping terrorists. I think he just thought of the money and didn't ask any questions."

"Sadly, my dad's always been greedy for money and has always had a terrible temper."

"I know Kevin has behaved badly," Eleanor added, "but one day I might find it in my heart to forgive him. There's always been a strange sort of tie between us, I can't deny that."

"You haven't got much family," said Jon, "so hang on to what you've got."

"Well, I've got more than you have," said Eleanor sadly. "Oh, by the way Mrs. Charles should be here shortly. The hospital contacted her."

Hardly had she finished speaking, when the ward doors were flung open, and Mrs. Charles waddled in. "Kevin!" she called and rushed across the ward to his bedside. Then she stopped when she saw Eleanor. "What are you doing here?"

"Well, it's like this, mother," said Eleanor, calmly, "I was in the village as the ambulance was leaving so I rode alongside him. You see I wanted to be with my half-brother."

"So you know." Mrs. Charles said. She paused then added. "Well, it's good of you to care so as to come and see him like. Deep down he's a good lad. Ain't got the quality that you have, and Gawd knows he's been in a load of trouble but he's my son and... and... I love him." She sniffed, then sighed. "Guess I should say sorry to you for not bringing you up, but well what with three other kids you wouldn't've had much of a life. And what with Dickie marrying into quality – your step mother was dead posh

- I thought you'd be better off with them. And you've turned out alright if I may say so. Yep, any mother would be right proud of you.

She paused for a moment to arrange her vast bulk into the only available chair and then added, "I wanted to tell you sooner but your Dad threatened me if I told you. Kevin too. Any way let me see my son, the poor darling."

Eleanor looked at her mother. She was hopelessly overweight. Wobbles of fat were inadequately cased in a short flowery sleeveless dress which she was wearing despite the cold weather. Her bare legs as large as tree trunks were lardy and pale. The chair she was sitting on was not up to the job of supporting her bottom which spilled over the sides. Her face was lined, and pallid, no doubt due to poor diet and stress.

Eleanor was suddenly overcome with emotion. It seemed preposterous that the slim pretty Eleanor could have a mother, so different, but this was her real mother. Despite everything, she leant over and gave her a hug.

Mrs. Charles quivered, and a tear rolled down her face

"There, there dear," she said, "life's been tough, what with all them kids, and no money but there wasn't a day that went by that I didn't think of you and wish you were part of your real family. I hope we'll see more of you and you can meet your brothers properly."

"Yes, I would like that," said Eleanor.

"Here let me take his hand now, love. He's still unconscious so maybe it ain't worth being with him, but still who knows maybe he can hear us but can't talk back."

Eleanor let Mrs. Charles take her place as chief hand holder, using her free hand to stroke his forehead. Eleanor gazed at his pale face. What will he be like when he wakes up? Will he have anything to do with me? Can I really be a sister to him? And what about my other half-brothers? It's all going to be very awkward.

Jonathan was getting restless. Like many who have never had a day's illness in their lives, he had a dislike of hospitals and could not see the point of a bedside vigil for an unconscious Kevin whom he actually did not like very much.

"Come on," he said, "let's go. No point in staying here. Could be days before he wakes up and Mrs. Charles is doing an excellent job. Give her your mobile number and she can ring you if he regains consciousness."

Eleanor, tired and emotional, silently assented, and, after phone numbers had been exchanged, they said their goodbyes and left the hospital.

Chapter Twenty

The next two days passed relatively peacefully. Eleanor refused to see her father, who was briefly held at Beckton police station before being whisked off to London for more questioning.

Jonathan wanted reassurance that they were now safe from the terrorists. He rang his uncle, who promised to ring back once he had found out what was going on. When his uncle finally returned the call, Jonathan was puzzled by his reply.

"They assured me they had the situation under control and were monitoring suspected terrorist activity in the Beckton area. They also said I should reassure you that, whatever happens, you shouldn't worry."

'Whatever happens'? What did they mean by that? Was something going to happen? The secret services were never ones to word replies carelessly. Jonathan began to worry all over again.

******

It was Friday lunch time when Eleanor got the news that Kevin was now sitting up in bed and could take visitors. Jonathan drove her to the hospital and waited in the hospital reception so she could be alone with her half-brother.

An hour or so later, Eleanor returned from her visit looking cheerful. "We had a longish chat," she said. "I think he'll behave better now he has me as a sister to make sure he keeps on the right side of the law. He's still very weak, but the doctors reckon he can be discharged in the next day or so."

"Great news, then," said Jonathan, "and I think you're right. I suspect that most of his bad behaviour was just that he was bitter about your family, and his, for the way they hushed you up, and for the snobbery of it all. Once the dust has settled, I think it will be brilliant. You'll get to know a whole new family."

They got in the car and soon were on the road back to Skandlebury. It was a pleasant, bright, sunny day, although it was a little cold. It was always a pleasure to drive on this quiet road through pretty countryside. Soon they arrived at the Forestry Commission woodlands on the outskirts of Skandlebury. The woods came right down to the road on both sides. There was a layby where generations of villagers and visitors parked their cars to go for a picnic, or a walk in the woods. It was at this point that they noticed a black Range Rover, headlights on full beam, approaching them at speed. Instead of passing them it braked and turned sharp right blocking the road. Three men leapt out of the car, guns pointing at them.

"Put your car in the layby!" yelled one of the men, and, rigid with shock for a moment, Jonathan had no option but to obey.

"Now get out! Hands on heads!" ordered the evident leader.

The two meekly obeyed, too shocked to even think of resisting. One of the men tied Jonathan and Eleanor's hands behind their backs. "Scream and we gag you!" shouted one of the men as they were flung roughly into the back of the Range Rover.

It was all over in seconds and Jonathan and Eleanor lay helpless in the capacious boot of their captors' car, as it sped off to an unknown destination.

Jonathan sensed they were heading back towards Skandlebury and this was confirmed by Eleanor who told Jonathan they had just gone over a particular bump in the road near the village green, which as a cyclist, she knew only too well.

Shortly afterwards the car drew to a halt. The boot was flung open. They were ordered to get out of the car. To their amazement they realised they were at the castle, in the visitors' carpark. However, a notice on the fence announced the closing of the castle for repairs. Jonathan doubted there was any truth in this.

They were pushed, stumbling, across the tarmac and up a flight of steps which took them up to the motte. They were led around the side of the keep to the forbidding stone walls of the main castle which towered above them. They came to a stop outside a door into the stone building. One of the men had a key with which he unlocked a door and the two were pushed through.

They found themselves in a small room with rough stone walls. Barred, glassless windows high up let in daylight and air, but the room looked gloomy and unused. Their hands were untied, and the men then left without a word, locking the door behind them.

They sat in the corner of the room in shocked silence, stunned by the speed of events.

"So much for police protection," said Jonathan bitterly. "What the hell's going to happen next?"

Eleanor answered in a small voice. "I don't know, but whatever happens I don't think it'll be good."

"We must stay positive," said Jonathan, "the local police and the secret service know about the plot. It will be foiled, I'm sure."

"Yeah," said Eleanor, "but what about us? They don't know we're here. The plot might be stopped but we could be dead by then."

Jon didn't reply. In his heart he knew she was probably right.

"I've visited the castle a few times," Eleanor said, "but I've never seen this room."

"I studied this castle when doing my degree. This room's newer... probably a 19th century addition – a storeroom, or something. It's been built in stone, in keeping with the rest of the castle."

Eleanor went over to the window, standing on tiptoe to look out. "There's a ditch down there," she said, "no way to get out here. Must be a 20 metre drop!"

On the castle wall was a projection of stone as if built around a giant pipe. Jon laughed. "This room was added at the bottom end of the garderobe or latrine," he said. "Behind this wall, the sewage from the lord and lady's chamber or solar would empty out into the moat. This would have been about the only place for a storage building and there's only just enough room for it."

Having completed the inspection of their prison they both made themselves as comfortable as possible on the stone floor, Jonathan sitting on a crumbling sandstone brick and Eleanor on the ground her knees drawn up to her chin.

They were silent for a while each absorbed in their own thoughts. The truth of the awful predicament they were in was dawning on Jonathan. The terrorists were going to involve him in an act too awful to contemplate, in which many innocent lives could be lost, not to mention the King's. To obey them would mean certain death for him and many others; to disobey, perhaps by taking an opportunity to escape, would imperil the life of

Eleanor, whom he loved to distraction. Worse than her losing her life would be the terrible torture and indignities the vengeful terrorists could inflict on her. He was angry and frustrated at the inactivity of the authorities whom they had notified and warned of the impending attack. He also felt his lack of self-control was responsible for Eleanor being captive. If they had kept their distance, as he had earlier resolved to do, it would just be him sitting on the floor of this dingy castle room.

Eleanor was thinking similar gloomy thoughts but hers were centred on how much she loved Jonathan. She couldn't contemplate life without him. They had spent so little time together. She was dimly aware that she might suffer at the hands of the terrorists, but the sheer horror of what they might do had not yet dawned on her.

It was Eleanor who eventually broke the silence.

"You know," she said, her voice quiet, "I used to dream of having Famous Five type adventures, where being locked in a ruined castle seemed to be nothing more than an unexpected inconvenience." She smiled wanly and hugged her knees. "I think this has cured my desire for adventure. Somehow the baddies in the Famous Five books were a pale reflection of the lot we're dealing with. They were usually smugglers or something. They wouldn't plot to kill the King and the Five never seemed to be in mortal danger."

"Chin up," said Jonathan trying to sound breezy and confident but failing dismally. "We'll find some way out, I'm sure. The opportunity will present itself. When I'm gone you must try to escape, call for help or something. Someone may hear you. Maybe try and loosen the bars or do something. Anything. I think tomorrow I'll be taken away as its Saturday. I'll do everything I can to try and escape. I refuse to be involved in this dreadful crime. My army training may give help, but I don't want you to suffer at their hands."

Eleanor gazed around the room. The walls seemed solid, unyielding and featureless apart from the garderobe pipe. Although the door was not particularly robust, it would be strong enough to resist any attempt by the two of them to break it down. The barred windows offered no help to the would-be escapee and even if she could loosen the bars as Jonathan suggested, the windows were too small and high up to wriggle through, slim though she was.

She sank back into despair. This was hopeless. The stone wall of their prison seemed impenetrable. The place for their imprisonment had been chosen precisely because it offered no obvious means of escape.

Eleanor suddenly had a glimmer of an idea, but there was no chance of Jonathan benefitting from her proposed method of escape due to his size - and the chances of its success were small. She decided to keep it to herself, but it gave her hope. It would be enough to ward off the black cloud of despair that was threatening to overwhelm her. She also had great faith in Jonathan and his ability to escape. She hoped his resourcefulness would see him through.

"Don't worry about me," she said "I'll be fine."

Jonathan, was relieved to see Eleanor looking less miserable.

They sat in silence for a few moments until Jonathan said. "Ellie, I don't know much about you and your family apart from your unorthodox background. What were you like as a child?"

She smiled. "My life up until I met you was quite dull. I spent some time in London with Mum, or should I say stepmum, and the rest down here. I suppose I had the best of both worlds really: all the stuff you can do in London like going to the theatre, or shopping, as well as seeing the sights, but I spent many weekends down here with my dad, and as I grew older my life was more centred round my horse. I begged my parents to let me go to school down here so I could be near my horse, Bluebell. Poor Bluebell died a year ago and now I have Captain, as you know. It was an awkward arrangement, but my parents took it in turns to stay in Skandlebury to look after me. When I think back it was very kind of them but given the secret they were keeping maybe it was guilt. I saw London less and less. It was funny because my sister is the opposite. She loves London and finds the countryside dull."

Eleanor stood up and stretched. The hard stone floor was uncomfortable. "When I was small, I always had my head stuck in books. My Mum's Enid Blytons and any other books I could lay my hands on. I loved Charles Dickens and Tom Sawyer and Huckleberry Finn and other classics as well. Hence the English Lit. Degree. I was a dreamy awkward child and apart from a few friends from school, like Bessie at the tea shop, I loved my own company. Maybe this was because I had an awkward relationship with my dad and I saw my mum less and less. She had a career in the city and as her responsibilities increased while we were growing up, she could not afford to spend much time with us. I suppose I had a less than ideal childhood but both my dad and stepmum were not really cut out to be parents. They were too wedded to their jobs. Besides, I think my dad didn't care for me too much because I reminded him of who my real mum was."

Jonathan went to contradict her but Eleanor cut across him with a small smile. "Don't worry, I'm not going to get all emotional. People have far worse deals than me in life. By the way," she added, "presuming we get out of this awful mess, what about us. Do you want kids?"

Jonathan smiled at her typical bluntness. "Yes, I suppose so. Let's just hope we live that long!"

Eleanor burst into tears and the next few minutes or so were spent by Jon comforting her.

The evening wore on endlessly. Finally, exhausted and stressed out Eleanor fell into a fitful sleep her head in Jonathan's lap. Jonathan nodded off too, his head resting against the hard stone wall.

Dawn finally arrived, grey fingers of light filtering through the small windows. As the light became stronger they both woke up. Jon was instantly alert as he had slept the lightest. Eleanor, on the other hand, woke gradually and groggily, emerging slowly from unconsciousness.

The minutes ticked by and soon sunlight was streaming through one of the barred windows, warming their chilled bodies. They could hear the dawn chorus, the business of spring continuing, regardless of the suffering of the two locked in the castle. Jon envied the carefree birdsong and tried not to think that this might be the last time he would hear this joyful sound.

In the light of early morning, Eleanor's optimism had evaporated somewhat but the germ of her plan kept her from despair. Jonathan, who had a dull but persistent headache from his uncomfortable night, was silent.

Eventually he said: "Something's been bugging me. How did they get the key to the castle? I mean you can't just walk into the castle and demand it."

"Nawaf," replied Eleanor gloomily. "Now he's cricket captain he's got status in society. Or maybe he has a friend in the castle. Either way to obtain the key would be simple for the likes of Nawaf."

"You're probably right," Jonathan replied, and the conversation tailed off.

They sat for a while in mutual misery, clinging to each like the survivors of a shipwreck. They were too numb to tell how much time had passed.

Eventually the silence was broken by the sound of heavy footsteps and the turning of the key in the lock. The heavy wooden door was unceremoniously flung open. They were almost relieved that the agony of waiting was over.

Two men entered. One of them, whom Jon recognized as Khalid, said immediately, "Let's get this straight. Jonathan, you're coming with us and you, bitch, are staying here. If you try to escape," he continued addressing Jonathan, "we'll find you and kill you. And then we'll kill your girlfriend, but we might have a bit of fun first." He leered lustfully at the pretty, slim figure of Eleanor dressed in tight jeans and a pink tee-shirt.

His colleague laughed and said: "Get up, we have to go now!"

Khalid was a short, thickset, balding man, with a sloping Neanderthal forehead and thick lips. His very appearance portrayed him as an uneducated brutish foot soldier of the cunning and manipulative leader of the terrorist cell. His colleague was not much better. He was of Slavic appearance with pronounced cheekbones. He had a broken nose and chipped front teeth, the product of a previous fight. He was fit and muscular, whereas Khalid was flabby and out of shape. Jonathan remembered the latter panting with his exertions in the woods a few days ago in their abortive first attempt to capture him.

He was pulled to his feet roughly and bundled out of the door.

"I love you!" Jon said as he was shoved out the door.

"Shut up!" snarled the Russian, "you made a big mistake when you messed with us!"

"Yeah," chipped in Khalid, clearly the subordinate to the masterful Russian, "I've always said it was a shame we didn't finish you off when we killed your father. Still, revenge feels good. I've spent years in prison, thanks to you."

Jonathan said nothing. He was shaking with anger; an anger that seemed to clear his brain and renew his determination to thwart the terrorists' plans.

He was half pushed, half dragged across the empty visitor car park and thrown into the back of the waiting Range Rover.

Eleanor, meanwhile, buried her face in her hands and sobbed.

Chapter Twenty-One

Crainscombe-on-Beck is a picturesque village set at a ford on the river of that same name. Whitewashed thatched cottages line a single street, down which a stream rushes on its way to the larger river. Pretty stone bridges arch over the stream at intervals, providing villagers with access to their houses from the street. Here the river Beck reaches its final phase having begun as a spring in distant hills, progressed to a fast-moving torrent, and then slowed to a lazy wide river, before its entry into the sea some 20 miles away. The unusually heavy rains of winter and early spring had swollen the river. It now coiled like an angry snake past the village.

Jonathan was puzzled. He had assumed they would be heading to Beckton, but instead they left Skandlebury in the opposite direction and drove through countryside to Crainscombe. The car sped through the village then took an uneven track alongside the river. It bumped and rocked over the rough ground for what Jonathan guessed was about a mile, but it may have been more. The track eventually petered out and they slowed down.

The car stopped at the banks of the river. Jonathan was bundled out and taken down to the riverside where a motorboat was tied to a makeshift mooring post. A couple of men were sitting on the edge of the boat, their legs swinging over the side. Jon recognised one of them as Khalid's companion from the woods a few days ago. He presumed it was Fahad. For a moment Jon considered wrenching free from Khalid and the Russian's grasp and taking his chances in the fast-flowing river, but, as if sensing his thoughts, he felt their grip on his arms tighten.

As Jon and his captors drew near to the boat, Nawaf appeared from below deck and called out to his men. They stopped their conversations and faced their leader. "Everything is going well. Omar's work on the bomb is going to plan and it is nearly ready. No one suspects an attack from the river; the security forces are anticipating problems on land. If we leave at 10.20, we should, by my calculation, arrive at the opening ceremony at the scheduled time of 11am precisely. And what a ceremony it will be! Britain will pay for the imperial mess it made of the Middle East, for its support of Israel, and for killing Muslims. And my friend Jon here, Skandlebury's gifted cricketing all-rounder, will also pay for his meddling, which nearly destroyed our little band of brothers."

The men clapped and cheered as Jonathan was pushed on to the boat. Nawaf addressed him: "So, this is what is going to happen," he hissed. "In a moment we will tie you up. I, personally, will guide the boat to within sight of Beckton and the wharf. I will leave, as I have no wish to be blown up, after fixing the accelerator on fast and you, the King, and the cream of local society, will all be blown to hell."

"Well don't expect me to set off the bomb," said Jonathan, trying to sound brave.

"Oh, don't you worry my friend," laughed Nawaf, "you can go to hell with a clear conscience. The bomb will be set off by a mobile phone in the hands of a colleague on shore. However, any attempt to escape or sabotage our efforts and your girlfriend is in big trouble."

Jonathan was roughly bound with rope around his arms and legs and left sitting on the deck alone. The men on deck left and sat on the grass in the sun. Nawaf disappeared below deck and Jonathan could hear the faint sound of a conversation. It was strangely peaceful; the sunshine was warm on his skin, the birds sang their hearts out, and the trees, freshly clothed in spring green were a picture. The river, deep and swift, caused the boat to bob slightly. Jonathan felt numb. He was tempted to give up, but after a while began to pick at the knots that tied his ankles. After some effort he managed to loosen the tight ropes slightly, but progress was slow. He wasn't sure what he would do if he succeeded in freeing himself, fully aware that any escape attempt could have unpleasant consequences.

Jonathan was stunned at the fiendish brilliance of the plot. To use a boat as a remote-controlled bomb was ingenious. All the security officers on land could not stop it! He could see no way out. For him it was a one-way trip to an inevitable, violent death.

Eventually Nawaf appeared with Omar, a short man with tight curly hair and a flat nose. He left the boat and joined the other men. Nawaf was exultant. "It's all ready," he said, and the men cheered. "You must all leave and wait for me at the hideout. I will let you know how it goes. Although," he laughed, "you'll probably hear the bang!"

The men cheered and then clambered into the Range Rover and drove off, the tyres skidding on the muddy ground.

Jonathan and Nawaf were alone in the boat.

Nawaf said nothing as he fired up the engine and the boat began its mathematically calculated last journey down the River Beck, its engine propeller churned the water, leaving a foamy trail. He sat at the wheel keeping the boat straight without so much as glancing at his victim.

It was on the sun dappled river, about half a mile downstream, that Jonathan finally gave up hope. A snowy white swan with her cygnets hidden in her feathers sailed majestically alongside the boat, and a gentle breeze blew blossom from a wild cherry tree onto the river, where the petals floated downstream like a fleet of tiny white coracles. A song thrush trilled its happiness from the top of a willow tree and a water vole bustled busily along the bank. Jonathan saw the idyllic scene with a new intensity. He could see the bright green reeds under the clear water, being pulled by the current, he saw a damsel fly darting here and there like an electric blue needle, and a robin alighting on a tree branch. Even the dandelion flowers, usually unnoticed, seemed to glow a rich burnished gold in the sunlight. It was as if nature was putting on a final display at its exuberant best, just for him.

Yet, amidst all this beauty, the impending cataclysm seemed impossible to contemplate and his sheer powerlessness to prevent it was slowly driving him insane. He struggled uselessly against the knots. After initially giving him a little slack, they were now unyielding.

Nawaf, meanwhile, sat rigid and still at the wheel of the boat, not even glancing at his victim. He was concentrating solely on steering the boat down the river to its deadly target.

Fifteen minutes to go.

His whole soul revolted at the idea of dying. He had just found love, and his life had taken on a purpose, and now it was to be senselessly cut short. He thought of Eleanor, that beautiful girl who had been by his side and was now likely to be killed. He bitterly regretted his foolishness at entering a relationship that put her life in mortal danger. What would his father think? A fearless man who lost his own life to save others and he, a selfish idiot, who should have done more to protect her.

Jon felt the beating of his heart ticking the seconds of his life away...

******

Eleanor, meanwhile, spent several minutes in abject hopelessness, first sobbing and then just sitting, hugging her knees. Separated from Jonathan, she now felt completely vulnerable and alone. The gnawing anxiety over what was happening to the man she loved added to her own predicament. It was the 'not knowing' that made the situation infinitely worse. On top of that she could add physical discomfort. She had a headache, a raging thirst and an empty feeling in the pit of her stomach.

All thoughts that her relationship with Jon had been rushed and things should slow down had left her. The intensity of their experiences had forged a deeper bond and it was a bitter irony that, despite all that, their futures now looked hopeless.

She had to snap out of it. It was time to put her plan into action. She forced herself to her feet and looked around her. The empty room was the same as it had been yesterday, except sunlight was pouring through the tiny high-up window which was too small for anyone to pass through. Bits of masonry and rock, presumably from the crumbling keep, lay on the floor. The tube-like garderobe was where her eyes finally settled. Could she climb up there? It was narrow and ran right to the floor, but the stones looked loose around the bottom. If only she could escape and warn the police...

Her heart beating fast, she eventually plucked up the courage to go over to the garderobe pipe to investigate. She began, at first tentatively, and then with an almost manic vigour, pulling and pushing one stone that seemed looser than the others, onto which her fingers could get a purchase. It began to move. She continued, wobbling it violently. She felt more movement. It was exhausting work, but she was encouraged to see little bits of mortar falling to the floor. Half an hour went by and the brick finally gave in. She was able to remove it. The next stone was much easier to move. There was now a significant gap and gradually she pulled away the stones, around the bottom of the pipe. She used the loose stones to hammer at the fixed ones until eventually she had created a big enough gap for her to slip into the garderobe pipe. Although the room was cool, she was perspiring profusely. Her nails were all ripped and bleeding, her arms and shoulders ached, and she was covered in dust, but she felt triumphant.

At last she was ready. She lay on her back and wriggled like a limbo dancer, through the gap into the garderobe pipe. Eleanor was slim enough to eventually stand upright in the dark, dank interior. As she had anticipated, the walls on the inside were rough and there was just enough room to reach up and find a handhold. She pulled herself up and found purchase for her feet, between the two sides of the chimney-like structure. She made slow but steady progress upwards...

******

His heart racing, Jonathan felt weak. The landscape was now spinning before his eyes. He could see houses up ahead. They had reached the outskirts of Beckton. Only a few minutes now.

Overwhelmed with a sudden terror, he began tugging furiously at the knots, screaming.

Then everything went blank.

It was in this semi-conscious state he dreamed he heard a voice say: "Here let me help you with those knots." Someone was sawing through the ropes.

"You poor fellow," said Nawaf, "you've been through hell. No time now for explanations right now. I'm just going to guide the boat into the bank here. There's a jetty. We'll get off the boat there."

Jonathan was held as he stumbled from the boat. This was no dream. The panic and blind terror slowly began to dissipate, replaced instead by a quiet bewilderment. He was led, still not fully aware of his surroundings, to a nondescript grey car. Gently, Nawaf escorted Jon into the passenger seat, where he slumped unmoving. As Nawaf got into the driver's seat his phone rang.

"Yes?" he said.

"What! How long have we got?"

His face was pale. "We must get to the castle. We've only five minutes, max. The gang have all been rounded up, but Khalid's escaped, God knows how, and we think he might be heading that way. I pray to God we get there before he does."

Jonathan, who was still trying to cope with this incredible turn of events, had never been driven so fast in his life. The hedges of country lanes flashed by in a green blur and Jonathan, although secured with a seat belt, was tossed around like a sack of flour as they hurtled towards Skandlebury castle.

Chapter Twenty-Two

Eleanor felt frustrated. Her progress had been halted by a piece of jutting wall, almost at the top of the garderobe and she could make no further progress. She felt fairly safe there, having armed herself with a small rock with which she hoped she could repel anyone trying to get to her. Gravity was on her side too and, with that brick resting in her lap, she felt more confident. She must have been at least 12 metres above the room. Freedom was only a few metres further on. She managed to wiggle into a relatively comfortable position and waited.

Time ticked on and Eleanor wondered what was happening to Jonathan. Would she be able to hear an explosion five miles away? The explosion would of course end any hopes that he was still alive. But all was quiet and nothing disturbed the peace of the ancient castle. Had he escaped? As the seconds ticked by, Eleanor's hopes rose. If he had it wouldn't be long before he would come to release her. She dreaded the alternative but, armed with a brick and high above her prison cell, she felt almost secure.

Then she heard a noise. It sounded like a car drawing up outside. Eleanor's heart beat faster. Was it Jonathan? If it was him he had been quick. She heard a fevered fiddling of a large key in the lock then a loud click. Was it Jonathan? She held her breath as the rusty door creaked open. There was a pause. Whoever was down below was obviously puzzled.

"Where are you, bitch?"

Eleanor froze.

She recognized the hate filled voice of Khalid.

She heard his feverish searching and cursing. It was some moments before Khalid realised she had escaped up the garderobe, the broken stone and the hole giving her away.

"You up there?" he called. "Come down, or I shoot!"

Eleanor flattened herself against the wall, hoping any bullets would fly past her or be deflected by the many protrusions of the uneven wall.

Looking down, she could just see a faint speck of light as Khalid's hand appeared holding the gun, followed by his head.

He was too large to climb up after her.

"So," he sneered, "you couldn't make it all the way up. You'd better come down then. As you can see I have a gun and I rarely miss." There was a pause. In the silence, Eleanor could hear Khalid's heavy, asthmatic breathing "This is your last warning. Come down or I shoot. I'm going to have my fun with you, you little whore."

Eleanor said nothing but pressed her body harder against the wall.

The sound of the shot reverberated throughout the castle. Eleanor screamed. She felt the bullets heat as it flew past her ear and smashed into the projection that had been impeding her upward progress. She was showered with dust and shards of stone. She wasn't hurt, and the spent bullet rebounded harmlessly off the wall of the garderobe above her head.

"Ok, ok!" she screamed, "I'm coming!"

Eleanor had to position herself in the middle of the pipe, for accuracy, and couldn't risk another shot. She manoeuvred herself into the centre and then opened her legs. The rock resting on her lap fell. Almost immediately, there was a yell and then silence. She peered somewhat tentatively down the shaft and thought she could make out Khalid's head. It was not moving.

Cautious, she began her descent, her trembling legs making progress slow. There was still no movement from below.

She heard another sound. Another car.

Surely this must be...

"Eleanor! Eleanor!" came a voice that was both dearly familiar and welcoming.

"I'm up the garderobe!" she yelled, "I'm coming!"

Her heart leapt with joy, overwhelmed with relief. Reassured that it was Jonathan, she quickened her descent.

Eventually she squeezed past Khalid's body, disgust rising in her throat as she was forced to rub past him.

She eased her way out of the hole and, on seeing Jonathan, rushed into his arms.

No words were needed as they experienced the uncontrolled joy of being reunited again. She didn't notice Nawaf standing by; all she was conscious of was the reassuring feeling of her lover's body pressed against hers, his beating heart against her chest.

It was some time before they disentangled themselves and it was Jonathan, ever the spell breaker, who spoke first.

"You look filthy," he said.

Eleanor laughed, her voice shaky. "So would you, if you'd been stuck up a medieval toilet for ages."

Eleanor noticed Nawaf. "What's he doing there?"

"Nawaf's not a terrorist," said Jon, quickly, "he's with the secret service." He looked at Khalid, who was still lying on the ground his head near the garderobe. "Gosh! Look what you've done to Khalid. I'd feel sorry for him if he wasn't such a murdering bastard."

Chapter Twenty-Three

They didn't have to wait long before an ambulance and several police cars drew up. Nawaf, who had stood silently by whilst Eleanor and Jonathan were reunited, went to the police car to explain the situation.

"We'll all need to go to the police station to make formal statements," said Nawaf when he returned, "but in the meantime I'll take you to hospital as a precautionary checkup. You're both in shock so I think the statements can wait."

Eleanor, like Jonathan, was finding it difficult to accept Nawaf as their unlikely saviour.

"I think you owe us an explanation first," said Eleanor, "because right now I see you as the murderer of Jon's parents, rather than the one who just saved his life."

"You're both in shock," said Nawaf, as he started the car. "I think you should go to hospital first. On top of that Eleanor, you have cuts and grazes that should be attended to."

"We need an explanation!" Jonathan shouted. His face was red, livid with the fury that had been building up since the overwhelming feeling of relief had subsided. "We have just been through hell and you, secret service or not, MURDERED MY PARENTS! I saw you do it!"

There was silence after this outburst and a look of pain registered on Nawaf's face.

"Well, I suppose," said Nawaf with forced calm, "an explanation might help you. Look, let me take you back to your home, Jonathan, and I'll explain everything. Suffice to say for now: I had no part in killing your family. Then I'll take you both to the hospital."

Jonathan didn't reply. They drove the short journey from the castle to Jonathan's home in silence.

Soon they were ensconced in the squashy sofas of Jonathan's lounge, drinking hot sweet tea and hungrily eating cheese sandwiches, prepared with remarkable speed and efficiency by Nawaf. Sir Lancelot quickly selected Nawaf's lap and jumped up, purring. He circled around a bit before settling down. Nawaf did not react to this distraction except to smile briefly and then stroke the cat rhythmically.

"Well?" said Jonathan. There was a heavy note to his voice, "I was only ten, but the picture of your face staring at me with wild eyes as I clung to my dead mother is not one I will forget easily. One thing I do know is that I'll take a hell of a lot of convincing that you didn't pull the trigger."

"Me neither," said Nawaf, and his voice seemed to contain a world of regret. "I too have that day engraved in my memory. Here, drink some more tea. It will do you good."

Silence followed as they sipped their tea. And then Nawaf spoke.

"I'll start from the beginning, and please believe me, what I am telling you is the complete truth.

"I was just 17 at the time of your family's murder, Jonathan. I was a tall gangly youth, a bit immature, and naïve too as I knew very little of life save for the small village in the desert I grew up in. My best friends were Khalid and Fahad who were older than me, but much shorter. It was my height that made villagers believe I was the leader of our little group, whereas in fact it was Khalid. We did everything together and got into a lot of mischief but we never hurt anyone. A year before the attack on your family they got radicalized; how I am not sure - most likely online – and they would preach to me with ardent enthusiasm, the need to fight against the enemies of Islam. They emphasized jihad or holy war against infidels, which not only meant non-Muslims but also the ordinary peace-loving ones like myself who would normally never hurt a fly. They singled out the west, and Britain in particular, for their hatred and had become involved with a terror group who took Al Qaeda as their inspiration."

"OAK," muttered Jonathan, bitterly.

Nawaf ignored the interruption and continued: "They were part of a larger gang that blew up a western hotel and assassinated prominent politicians. These attacks were of course reported in the international press and the two revelled in the notoriety they had achieved.

"I was taken in by their eloquent and constant pleas to become, as they saw it, a soldier for Islam and that I would be instantly transported to paradise if I died for the cause. Eventually, mainly because I now believed in their cause, but also out of loyalty to my friends, I reluctantly agreed to join in with their schemes. I went on several so-called missions involving brick throwing and demonstrations outside the British or American Embassies. I now see they were just softening me up for a more bloody and violent enterprise. They explained that it was to intimidate a prominent employee at the British Embassy.

"They lied to me about the purpose of their mission. Your dad, as you know, was employed as a researcher at the Embassy but his main role was to gather intelligence on terrorism. He had eventually tracked down a member of our gang, who out of fear of torture, not that the British government at that time indulged in such things, blabbed. As a result, several gang members were arrested and imprisoned and, we believed, tortured.

This left Khalid and Fahad very angry, and very worried. They decided to target the person responsible for this, and they knew from a sympathetic embassy worker that it was your dad. They told me they were going to fire a few warning shots at their villa, and I agreed to accompany them, happy to spray a few bullets harmlessly at a villa wall."

Nawaf paused and took another sip of tea. Jonathan noticed that the hand holding the cup was shaking slightly. There was silence except for the ticking of the grandfather clock in the hall. They were listening with rapt attention.

"Your dad was impatient with the security precautions of a military compound and had chosen a villa on the edge of the city next to open desert. It had a high wall around it topped with barbed wire and round the clock security guards. This was deemed by the authorities to be adequate security. I think your father preferred to live amongst ordinary citizens, rather than in the 'Embassy bubble'. Unfortunately, this was his downfall as he could now be targeted much more easily.

"In fact, the family, that's you and your Mum and dad, had entered the gates, and were crossing the garden to the house, the maid and the driver as you know were also in the garden. The gates were wide open. Seizing the opportunity this coincidence afforded, they shot the security guard and ordered me to enter the gates with them. Then the carnage began. You must believe me I was too shocked even to fire my gun and in the horror of that awful massacre any belief in radicalism died.

"Fahad shouted to me, as I was the last to leave that compound, 'Are they all dead?' and I said, 'I'll check'. I had spotted you clinging to your mother's skirt, and I went over to warn you to keep still, but your face was chalk white. You were in such a state of shock that I said nothing but confirmed to them that you were all dead. Those wild eyes you saw were not full of hate but shock."

Jonathan and Eleanor were clinging onto every word Nawaf said. He paused so that the enormity of what he was saying could sink in. "I'll get some more tea," he said in a low voice, and went to the kitchen.

Eleanor looked around the sitting room and noticed, for the first time, the picture on the sideboard. A laughing couple holding hands, with a camel apparently intruding. Eleanor didn't need to ask who the couple were. They were a tall dark-haired man and a slim, pretty, fair-haired woman each bearing some resemblance to Jonathan. Seeing what they looked like brought home anew the enormity of the tragedy that had befallen Jonathan. Nawaf returned with fresh tea.

"So," said Jonathan, slowly, at last convinced at Nawaf's sincerity, "I suppose you saved my life and for that I thank you." Nawaf refilled their cups, adding liberal doses of sugar, ignoring

Eleanor's protests that she didn't take sugar.

"Well, yes but since that day I've had to live with the guilt of what my gang had done to you, and I was determined to make amends. My first action was to ring the British Embassy and the emergency services and officers were soon on the scene. I surrendered to intelligence officials who took me to the Embassy for questioning. You also were taken back to the embassy. I told my interrogators all about the gang and Khalid and Fahad were arrested by the local police and, after a trial, jailed for ten years. They were lucky not to be executed but the judge was probably a sympathiser. It is difficult to get impartial justice in that region of the country where family loyalties and religious affiliations frequently override justice. They found out, while they were in prison, that you were still alive and assumed the information that led to their arrest had come from you, particularly as, in the subsequent hours, you were taken to the embassy and your villa searched. Even if they hadn't blamed you those two were of the sort that if one member of your family remained alive then the mission was incomplete, and they were duty bound to complete it. They never suspected me and were completely unaware I'd turned myself in."

"Well I did help a bit," said Jon, "I remember hearing my dad mention a possible location where the gang might be hiding, which I passed on, and I showed them how to get on to my dad's computer where they found other information."

"You were a great help, as the information that I could pass on was limited because they, like most terrorist cells, operated on a need-to-know basis. I knew very little about the group to which I had been recruited. Anyway, as you know, several years later they escaped from jail and were helped out of the country by the OAK network. They joined up with a gang who had members in the UK and was part of one of the most extensive terrorist networks affiliated to OAK.

"In the meantime, I joined MI6 and, based in the Middle East, I went on various undercover missions using my notoriety as part of the gang who murdered your dad as a ticket of acceptance to radical Islamists. As a result, several plots were thwarted without compromising my identity, including that well publicized failed plot to blow up a hotel in Jordan where the bomb failed to go off and the police chief mysteriously vanished.

"Interest now moved to Britain once MI5 learned the gang had affiliates there. My bosses at MI6 got me on a course of international relations at Cambridge, where I improved my English and learned to love cricket and all things British.

"I resumed my work in the Middle East, temporarily, and soon got word that Khalid and friends were planning to move to Britain to plot what they called a 'spectacular' on an as yet unknown target. They were still very bitter at what they perceived, in their twisted way of thinking, was your role in their downfall, and thought that maybe they could track you down in England.

"So once more I too returned to the UK on the trail of Khalid and friends. The intelligence agencies were aware of a gang already operating in the UK under the OAK umbrella, and were not surprised that Khalid and Fahad had joined them. The intelligence chiefs wanted to round up all the gang, rather like ensuring that a cancerous growth was completely removed. I managed to contact them too, and they welcomed me back with open arms as they respected my skills of planning and organization. Yes, Khalid and friends provided the hate and the fanaticism; I was the cool brain behind their schemes.

"I first suggested they drop all plans and concentrate on the big one. I suggested to them that they could assassinate the King on one of his official functions. At the same time, they could somehow involve you, Jon, in the attack, perhaps by forcing you to carry out a suicide bombing. I won acceptance of this plan. I heard the King was going to open a new shopping centre in Beckton as part of a regeneration plan, and when I told them they couldn't believe their luck that they'd be carrying out their plans near where you lived. They could coordinate their twin aims more easily. It also relieved me of the stress of trying to sabotage every plan involving loss of life. So, I hoped that concentrating on a 'spectacular' would actually save lives. They dropped their many bloodthirsty plots and concentrated on the big one. MI6 with MI5 hatched the scheme to attack the King at Beckton. To ensure there was no danger, his visit was scheduled an hour later than planned. In fact, he will be opening the Centre about now. Officials will apologize to the crowd for the delay but explained that the King had been temporarily indisposed.

"I managed to convince the terrorists to strike from the river and they were thrilled at the idea of putting you on the boat and killing you at the same time. The thought of you, their enemy, dying in the same explosion that would kill the King excited them. They saw it as a sort of poetic justice. Plans went ahead for the opening, and I gave them every assistance. The local police were informed and fully cooperated. To coordinate matters, I rented a house in Hangman's Lane and Fahad and Khalid also used it as a base. It is where I suspect the police are at this very moment, having rounded up almost the entire network. With your dad's cooperation, Eleanor, and with the information you gave us on the finance side we expect to make more arrests in London too. I also joined your cricket club, purely because I love cricket and the club were so impressed with my cricketing skills, learnt at Cambridge, that they asked me to be captain. I agreed to take over on the day of the friendly and poor old Jon, you had quite a shock. It was agreed rather hurriedly, so I could be in place for the start of the season. You missed the emergency meeting at which the decision was made, and I don't think your club thought to tell you. I'm not sure what you were doing. I think you were visiting your uncle? Anyway, I made sure the meeting took place while you were away." A smile flickered for a moment across Nawaf's otherwise serious face.

"So, how did you meet Bert, and why did you help him in his plan to get me 'busy'?" asked Jonathan.

Nawaf smiled. "This is where coincidences started."

"It was in Skandlebury, while having my car serviced that I met Bert. During conversations with him you cropped up. He mentioned that you were Skandlebury's best cricketer but had become insufferable lately, complaining of having nothing to do. To amuse him, I suggested you be involved in resurrecting the Frobisher case. You remember the case caused a huge stir in the village and everyone knew about it. By this time of course the inquest had passed a verdict of accidental death but I, like many, had doubts. I half had in mind that if you had something to do, I could keep you close. It had nothing to do with the terrorists, or so I thought. I had no idea that Fahad and Khalid were involved in a smuggling operation and storing stuff at the barn. I had not been briefed on their fund-raising methods and as I said terrorist cell members are told only what they need to know."

"I suppose the police cooperated in giving you the identity of D I Sims," said Jonathan.

"Yes, they pretty well did exactly what I asked of them, knowing I was in the intelligence services, and I used the genuine former DI Sims ID card. They even facilitated your imprisonment in the castle. My suggestion, I am afraid, as I wanted to know where they were going to keep you to ensure you came to no harm."

"We went through hell," burst out Eleanor. "Have you any idea what it is to be helpless, locked in a castle with no hope of getting out alive? What you did was... was cruel."

Nawaf poured out yet another cup of tea and again added several sugars. Jonathan put his arm around her. Sir Lancelot, tired of being constantly evicted from Nawaf's lap, resettled himself on Eleanor's.

"I am truly sorry. I could see no other way of getting the gang all together so we could arrest them in one fell swoop while they were actively carrying out an act of terror. I felt if we told you, you might give the game away, although your uncle dropped a hint when you phoned him. He, of course, had been in touch with us. We felt that in the long run your temporary discomfort was less important than making sure nothing went wrong in rounding up a sophisticated and determined terrorist gang who could cause all kinds of damage and loss of life."

"I must admit," said Jonathan, "that I feel a complete idiot. We should have guessed that something odd was going on when the police didn't seem to be interested in what we had to say. Also, where were you when they tried to capture me in the woods?"

"That was unscheduled," admitted Nawaf. "Those two idiots let their enthusiasm run away with them and they plotted on their own. They thought they might win my commendation too. This was not my plan. It was too soon. I wanted to minimise the time you would spend as prisoners. They had watched you run most mornings and took a chance. Well done for escaping, by the way."

Jon gave a weak smile. "It wasn't difficult. I don't think either of them had been in a forest before."

Nawaf nodded. "They showed surprising incompetence, but as I have heard it said, fanaticism is usually incompatible with common sense. I myself suffered the revulsion of having to plan a terrorist event with them and pretend to be as sick minded as they were. Still, I got my own back by treating them like dirt."

He paused for a moment as he recalled a whimpering Fahad struggling to get up after his thump in the face from Nikita, and then said, "Well, once again I am deeply sorry at the stress we caused you, but we rounded up a very dangerous gang. If they had managed to elude us, God only knows what havoc they could wreak."

"Why couldn't you have reassured me in the boat?" asked Jonathan." I was going through hell. I truly thought that I was going to die. Do you know what that feels like?"

"I suppose I could have reassured you," replied Nawaf, "but I was frightened you wouldn't believe me and, if I untied you, you might in rage or panic, attack me - I am no physical match for you. I suppose I was also terrified of anything going wrong."

Eleanor was clearly struggling to come to terms with all this, and forgiving Nawaf did not come easy, but as they talked into the evening, she gradually warmed to him and realised that he himself had been in real danger as a mole in the terrorist cell. He had come a long way from being a member of a bloodthirsty gang, as a vulnerable teenager. Any caution on his behalf, which led to greater stress for themselves, was justifiable.

Eleanor persuaded Jon and Nawaf that her cuts were superficial and, after baths and a microwaved meal, they both felt better. Nawaf suggested they spend a quiet day together tomorrow and official interviews and statements could wait until Monday.

Chapter Twenty-Four

"Let's go to church," said Eleanor, as they lay in bed that Sunday morning. Sir Lancelot was still sound asleep at the end of their bed. Sunlight was seeping through the gap in the curtains. It promised to be another warm day.

Jonathan grunted in reply. He had had a bad night, tossing and turning, as his mind went over all that happened to him. It seemed incredible that an ordinary, middle-class lad like himself, from a sleepy rural village should have his life inextricably bound up with a vicious terrorist gang from a hot desert, thousands of miles away. He felt better; the promise of a quiet day with Eleanor and a beautiful spring morning were restorative to him.

"I'll take that as a yes," she said briskly, leaping out of bed and putting on her dressing gown, "and I'll cook you breakfast."

"Er, thanks," he said, as Eleanor padded barefoot down the old oak stairs to the kitchen.

Jonathan suddenly sat up in alarm. Today was the first cricket match of the Sunday League. Skandlebury were playing Pobbleton in the match delayed by the foul weather. He had looked forward to this match for months. But now he felt he just could not face it. *Nawaf will have to do without me*, he thought. *I am sure he can make allowances for the fact that, only yesterday, I was totally certain that my life would end violently, being blown to pieces in a terrorist "spectacular". I think I am suffering from... what do they call it? Post-traumatic stress disorder?* There were times when even cricket had to take a back seat.

So much had happened over the past two weeks or so, some good and some bad, but they both needed time and a bit of normality to get over it. Maybe church was part of that normality, that recovery process.

Eleanor had been in good spirits that evening but her mood was brittle, and Jonathan felt she could snap at any moment. Again, normality and time could be the key to her recovery. He felt that, overall, she had coped with danger, indeed, mortal peril, better than he had.

Jonathan showered and dressed and joined Eleanor in the kitchen. Half an hour later, stomachs full of American style pancakes with maple syrup, which was Eleanor's favourite breakfast, they set off to the medieval church of St Michael and All Angels, which had been the centre of worship in Skandlebury for nearly a thousand years.

Their journey took them down School Lane to the centre of the village and across the green to the equally imaginatively named Church Lane where the square towered church was located.

As they crossed the green, they caught up with Mike Jones' wife, Ruth, trying to control her twin boys who, like puppy dogs, were continually trying to escape to release their boundless energy by running up and down the green, throwing sticks and wrestling on the dewy grass, dangerously close to the village pond.

Ruth, no doubt concerned at the state of their clothes by the time they got to church and worried they would fall in the pond, was trying somewhat unsuccessfully to control them. "Billy, come here!" she called, rather ineffectually. "Harry, get up off the ground, you'll ruin your trousers!"

She was an absent minded but well-meaning woman, quite attractive behind a rather wispy washed out exterior and a look of perpetual exhaustion. Her hair was a pale straw colour, and it was always trying to escape her attempts to harness it with pins and hair bands. As a result, she was habitually fending off a strand of hair that was determined to flop over her face. She was wearing a rather frumpy flowery dress, obviously handmade, and a white cardigan.

Eleanor liked Ruth and right now she represented down to earth normality. Ruth was one of those rare people who always believed the best in people. If her husband came in late on a Friday complaining of not feeling well, she would give him an aspirin and assure him that it was probably something he ate, despite him smelling of whisky.

Jonathan went on ahead, leaving the two women chatting. In front of the church, on a noticeboard, was a poster featuring an image of the risen Christ who proclaimed, "I am the Way, the Truth, and the Life". To Jonathan the picture was reassuring and comforting. He found a pew in the cool interior of the church. He bowed his head feeling anew the tension and fear of yesterday. As the sun emerged from a cloud, a beam of bright sunlight lit up the magnificent stained-glass window portraying St. Michael battling the dragon, illuminating it in stunning colours of red, green and gold.

Good defeating evil, thought Jon, and it came upon him in a sudden realisation that good was a greater power than evil, that evil would always eventually be defeated, and the One who was the way, the truth and the life had conquered death and evil, Himself. Tears filled his eyes: tears of relief and joy. A shaft of light had entered his soul. As he bowed his head, he sensed rather than saw Eleanor slip into the pew beside him and felt her soft lips press against his cheek. She sensed his epiphany and with the tenderness of a lover did not intrude.

Later in the day there was more good news. Skandlebury had thrashed Pobbleton by nine wickets. Jonathan was exultant but well aware that maybe there were more important things in life than cricket, although he would never dare disclose that view to his team

Lying in bed that night an old memory surfaced.

In the memory Jonathan is laughing happily, curly blond hair glowing in the sunlight, caught in a tangle by the light breeze. He is standing in front of a set of sticks that form a makeshift wicket and has just struck the ball over the whitewashed garden wall. "Six!" he cries, raising his bat in the air in triumph. His father runs to him and ruffles his hair. "Well done, son!" he says. His mother appears in the garden with a tray of biscuits and glasses of orange squash, and he runs to her triumphantly. "Mummy!" he cries "I got a six!" His mother says, "Well done darling", concentrating on trying not to spill the drinks.

They sit on the warm grass, where, nearby, a bougainvillea blooms extravagantly in bright purple. They munch biscuits and drink the squash while, high above them a hawk soars through the deep blue sky. Outside he knows is the harsh desert where dangers lie, but here he is safe.

Jonathan smiled, turned over, and fell fast asleep.

Epilogue

Two Months Later

The pub was hot and noisy. Empty beer glasses were scattered across the large oak table around which Nawaf, Mike Jones, Eleanor, Jon, and Mrs. Charles were sat. Kevin, Bessie, and Claire were also there. Bert joined them, pleased he had injected some excitement into his friend's life and no longer had to endure Jonathan's complaints of boredom over a lunch time pint. A half empty bottle of wine stood in the centre of the table next to a small bunch of red roses, freshly picked from the Puss-in-Boots garden.

There was a lot of laughter. Mike Jones had been laughing

at Jon and Eleanor's misfortunes and they had all joined in. Somehow in the jovial atmosphere, jokes about murderous sex sirens and medieval lavatories almost seemed in good taste.

Kevin was more subdued. After his release from hospital he had been prone to bad headaches but the doctors had reassured him that these would lessen in severity over time. Eleanor and Jon had taken a lot of time to get to know him and had ascertained correctly that a lot of his antisocial behaviour was down to his bitterness at being rejected by Eleanor's father. Jon had persuaded the landlord of the Puss-in-Boots to lift the ban and, so far, Kevin had not committed any transgression. He was due to appear in the magistrates' court in a week's time on charges relating to his van driving for the terrorists, but Jonathan was confident that he would be let off lightly, given the ordeal he had been through and the fact that Jonathan would act as a guarantor of his good behaviour. Blackmail charges had been quietly dropped.

Meanwhile Bessie was proudly showing off her ring. She had just got engaged to Kevin. The pub visit was by way of celebration of this event. "It was all a bit sudden," she giggled. "Kevin came into the teashop and, after drinking tea and eating a slice of chocolate cake, he got down on one knee and proposed. He had a red rose in one hand, and he looked so scared. Of course, I said yes. I'd known for some time we were supposed to be together."

Kevin had come a long way in a short space of time. In the

two months since his injury, he had done a lot of soul searching and decided that he could do no worse than settle down with a kind loving girl like Bess. Wanting to be jack-the-lad had made him eschew long lasting relationships, but after he had come out of hospital, he had gone straight to Bess, and they had started dating in earnest. With a steady girlfriend had come a secure job - as a driver for a luxury car hire company, which he was due to start once the doctor gave the all-clear. At Eleanor's insistence he had signed up for an accountancy course. His half-sister's mission to improve him amused him but he secretly welcomed this opportunity to use his considerable intelligence for good.

Eleanor had met other half-brothers and had struck up a close relationship with one named Carl, who proved to be a good friend and was also beginning to settle down. Bert had agreed to take him on as an apprentice at his garage. The other half brother, Pete, was still in prison and although Eleanor had visited him once, she found that visiting time was too short to strike up a meaningful relationship. The third had disappeared after a spell in prison and his whereabouts were unknown.

Mrs. Charles, sipping a glass of water, was looking forward to the wedding and devoting her time to preparing for it. So much so that her weight had been falling steadily. She was determined to look her best on the day of the wedding. Jon had paid his gardener to tidy up their garden and, with Mike, had helped redecorate the house in readiness. The vicar had managed to fit the couple in in September and time was very short. Eleanor had offered to rent out her dad's house to the newlyweds at a very competitive rate.

Nawaf was earnestly in discussion with Billy Landsman on cricket tactics. Under Nawaf's captaincy Skandlebury was flourishing at the top of the Sunday League, although Bellhinton with Alan Hardy as captain was a close second. Billy had only just joined and was showing promise as a batsman-cum-wicketkeeper. The two teams were due to play a friendly next weekend for the Edwin Frobisher Memorial Trophy.

Nawaf had become very close friends with Jon and, although he was away in London a lot on MI5 business, they met as often as they could, usually in the Puss-in-Boots. Eleanor had been to see her father once. He was due to spend the next five years in jail for causing actual bodily harm and charges relating to money laundering. His sentence had been reduced because of his valuable evidence that helped round up gang members involved in artefact smuggling and money laundering. He was truly sorry, he said, for his behaviour and he hoped that an anger management course would help. In the meantime, his wife was finalising divorce papers, her patience exhausted by his constant infidelities and his violent, criminal behaviour.

Jonathan and Eleanor had also got engaged so the pub meal was by way of a joint celebration. They were in no hurry to get married. Eleanor was due to start her English literature course in September which she was looking forward to and wanted to concentrate on that rather than the time-consuming arrangements for a wedding. Her sister frequently stayed with them, as did her mother, and Eleanor had come to terms with her parents' deception over her identity.

All her fears, about their whirlwind relationship, forged in a time of extreme peril, not being rock solid, had been banished. Jon was very attentive to her needs, and he remained madly in love with her, and she with him.

To Eleanor's relief, Khalid eventually recovered from his blow to the head. She didn't want to cope with the knowledge she had killed someone. He and the rest of gang were facing life in prison. As of course was Virginie.

The night wore on until, one by one, the members of the little group slipped away and only Jon and Eleanor remained. Jon had to settle the tab, having agreed to pay for everyone's drinks.

"What an eventful summer it's been," chuckled the landlord, "terrorism, murder, and fraud. Whatever next?"

Jon and Eleanor laughed despite the recent events being still very much alive in their memories. "Yes, whoever thought village life was dull?" Jonathan said.

Gary Lansdowne snorted. "I like dull. No more mayhem, please. And if you ever put your detective skills to the test again, I think your first case should be Mike. How does he manage to drink so much and stay upright? And why does darling Ruth put up with him?"

Outside, the warm midsummer night wrapped itself like a blanket around the village. Jonathan looked around as they paused on the threshold. Eleanor wrapped her arms around him as they began their walk home, sighing contentedly. Jonathan looked around at the peaceful scene savouring the scented air and taking in the dearly familiar village with its ancient church and castle, both dark outlines in the night sky. Opposite them, lights were going out as the villagers went to bed. Soon Skandlebury would slumber peacefully, as it had done for the last thousand years.

About The Author

David Munday is a retired teacher who lives in Devon with his wife, and their cat, Pumpkin.

He enjoys walking in the Devon countryside, is active in his local church, and spends far too much time playing word games.

He spent nine years teaching abroad, six of which were in the Middle East.

Printed in Great Britain
by Amazon